Legend Press Ltd, 51 Gower Street, London, WC1E 6HJ
info@legendpress.co.uk | www.legendpress.co.uk

First edition published by Copper Monstera in 2019 | Second edition
published by Blackbird Books in 2020, 593 Zone 4, Seshego, Polokwane
0742, South Africa

Print ISBN 9781915643629
Ebook ISBN 9781915643636
Set in Times. Printed in the UK by Severn Press
Cover design by Gudrun Jobst | www. yotedesign.com

Natasha Omokhodion-Kalulu Banda is a Zambian of Nigerian and Jamaican heritage. Her short stories have featured in various publications, including *Short Story Day Africa 2018* for 'Door of No Return', which was translated into Portuguese for Brazilian Journal *Periferias*. Her latest short story, 'Her Sweetie, Her Sugarcane' has been released in Harper Via's anthology *Reflections*. She is an alumni of Curtis Brown Creative's Breakthrough Course for Black Writers, and an MA candidate in Creative Writing at Kingston University London.

Natasha's first book, *No Be From Hia*, was selected as a Graywolf Africa Press finalist in 2019. Published in Zambia, it has gone on to markets in South Africa, Canada as well as the UK. She has served the Afritondo Prize judging panel in 2022.

This book I dedicate to God our Creator, the One who orchestrated all events in the universe to lead us to this very moment.

To my ancestors gone before me, to my children and generations to come – energy never dies.

PROLOGUE

MARGARET BUPE KOMBE
LUSAKA, ZAMBIA, 1967

MARGARET KOMBE STRETCHED HER hands through the dim evening light, fumbling for her hiding place. She paused to rub her temple. It throbbed, and lately, it never stopped. A protest march thundered through her head. Her fingers trembled along the edge of her afro, which had shrunk to a tight bed of knots. She wiped the beads of sweat from her forehead. Beneath her bed were secreted shampoo bottles from hotels around the world. They sat concealed in a domed wooden box passed on to her by her late mother. She opened one in haste, inhaling deeply before she took a swig of hard liquor. Finally, she felt brave enough to go into her walk-in wardrobe.

She slid into the sapphire blue stage dress given to her by Fabiola, the soukous dancing starlet from Congo's Léopoldville. The first time her husband laid eyes on the dress, it had mesmerised him. Fabiola's dark skin and large brown eyes had held every man who laid eyes on her in capture. Margaret had watched as Fabiola's thin waist, which could move in seven different directions, ensnared him. Margaret was not stupid – she was wise. A woman's success is that of her marriage and nothing else. She would never betray him. Her love would be enough to get through this. That, and one more drink.

Some of the small plastic bottles had vodka, a few had brandy, and others gin. Margaret had stopped caring what she drank long ago. She went back to the dressing table, tripping over the edge of the rug, to powder her slender face and line her eyes densely with kohl. She pressed scarlet lipstick to her lips, applying it thickly and slowly. Through bleary eyes that slanted upwards like pumpkin seeds, she placed that last touch of beauty on her face – a black spot to the left of her mouth, just the way her dancing counterpart did it.

From within her woolly, undefined mind she decided she'd call her babies the next day. She would speak to her children in good English. Maybe they would love her more; though she knew her baby Kabaso still fell asleep to the Bemba hymns she sung to him.

Margaret sighed. Thinking of her children coming home only once a year, every English summer, always brought a deep, exquisite pain. CJ, her first, was almost done with boarding school now, but it would still be some time before he returned home to Zambia from university in London. Stella, her middle child, was her father through and through; fierce and misguided. And her baby, Kabaso – she sniffed – he was only nine. She'd missed him terribly for two solid years.

'It is for the best,' her husband would say whenever she asked him. With his voice booming as he sat in his black leather recliner and his nose buried inside a gold-foiled volume from Kwame Nkrumah, he'd once firmly stated: 'The children should be educated in Britain if we want them to make it in the New World. That is why we spent so much time and sacrificed so much fighting for this country, so that we too could enjoy these benefits! One day, they can return to build their country and take over from where we will leave.'

A bass guitar and a piano played the prelude to trumpet notes from Miles Davis's 'Kind of Blue'. The music filled the bedroom. That was Bashi CJ's favourite music. He was Bashi CJ – or 'the father of' CJ – to her. But to the world, he was the great, honourable Charles Kombe. Maybe he would like it if he found her playing it for him; dressed beautifully, like his starlet.

She braided her hair in rough plaits and placed a blonde beehive shaped wig on her head. She looked at the pills on her table and shook a handful of shiny red capsules into her palm. She swallowed them with another drink. A warm glow spread outwards from her stomach. It was enough to numb the pain. She looked in the mirror and touched herself gingerly. Perhaps that was how Charles touched Fabiola. She clutched her womb as though trying to tear out fistfuls of flesh while returning the blank stare of her image.

Margaret glided through the hall with bare feet and stepped carefully down the stairs – the glamorous, sapphire blue train of her ballgown trailing behind her. Its cold silk hugged her skin softly. She paused, one hand holding the banister and the other touching her forehead. Sweat beaded on her lip.

She passed the indoor courtyard to the red brick veranda and down to the swimming pool. Perhaps a short dip in the water would give her some relief. She plunged her foot into the water. It was cool. Inviting. She felt dizzy, happy, and sad all at the same time. How could this be? She laughed at the irony of it all – perhaps this way, the gods would feel she shared their wicked sense of humour.

The world swam in Margaret's vision; a blur of blues and greens against the twisted silhouettes of rustling trees. She heard them whisper, laughing, nudging each other with murmurs of scorn and hisses of accusation. She looked up.

The world swung. She felt light; lighter than a leaf tossed on a breeze. For one beautiful moment, just after losing her balance, she seemed to hang in the air above the placid green water, like an angel. Her gown flowed gracefully behind her, obedient to the power of the warm night wind. She felt free, finally, like the earlier days from the mountain tops of Chinsali: rushing rivers gushing beneath her feet; rich verdant valleys rolling out to the skies before her to the point where the sky meets the land, the horizon where God can be found. That place where the goddesses rest their pestles against the skyline.

With a splash, she fell into the kidney-shaped pool.

Her eyes shut tightly as she sank slowly. Her dress tangled around her thin legs.

Water. It surrounded her. She moved her hands through it, searching for the surface, but she was so weak. She opened her mouth wide for air, kicked her legs, tried to climb.

Another deep gasp for air, and her face was smothered in fabric like a smoothed oval tarpaulin. The sapphire silk wrapped itself around her while the water spiralled her downwards, sinking her further into the wet abyss. She had never learned to swim.

*

In London, young CJ and his best friend, Abisola, clambered downstairs to see who was calling incessantly at such an ungodly hour. Mrs Ayomide had beaten them to it, and she crept out of the drawing room. She was sweating profusely, and her eyes were unsteady. 'CJ, your father is on the line for you'.

He took the handset and felt its cold coiling cable along his skinny arm. He turned away from the look on his friend's mother's face and inclined his head low, to the right, as though it would help him to hear the voice on the other side better.

Crackling static.

Silence.

'Good morning, sir,' he said, greeting his father, still wondering why he would call so early at his friend's home.

His eyes were pressed shut as he adjusted to the sunlight seeping in through the glass of the drawing room.

'CJ, your mother was found dead in the swimming pool this morning'.

CJ slumped onto the wooden cabinet behind him.

His father's deep baritone voice rolled through the phone line from the other side, distant and cold, like a dart to a board. He minced no words. 'I'm making arrangements for your flight. Please be ready for your pickup at four o'clock this afternoon and remember to thank the Ayomides for looking after you. Unfortunately, this is one of those times in life where we must stand strong, my son. Your siblings need not be disturbed by this news. Not a word to them until I say so – do you understand?'

'Yes, sir.'

'Your brother and sister will continue the term, and we will see them during the summer holidays as always.' The phone went dead with a click.

PART I

CHAPTER 1

MAGGIE OLUWASEUN AYOMIDE
LUSAKA, ZAMBIA, 1991

I WAKE WITH A start to the sound of adult voices in the corridor of our little flat.

My father's familiar bass voice and my mother's defiant responses reverberate through the thin walls. A third voice, my mother's friend from next door, Chonta, is pleading with my father. The commotion cannot be ignored. I remember where I am, and a heavy, sinking feeling opens in my heart, like an anchor dropping through deep water, farther and farther, until it plops at the bottom of a murky floor.

I have not seen my father since we left London, and that was a long time ago. I was still in grade one. After a long ride in a black cab behind red lights that blurred into snaky lines and a foggy smokescreen from exhaust pipes, Mum and I burst through the airport's doors and winded our way through the luminous jungle of Heathrow.

It was the middle of the night, and it seemed we ran and ran for miles. We were the last ones to get on the plane after Mum shouted at the red faced man who had hair plastered to his forehead. She shouted, and then she cried, and then she begged, and finally they opened the gate for us. I dropped my soft doll Eleanor because we had to hurry, and I've never seen her again.

I'm now in grade three, and I've almost forgotten the

rhythmic thump-thump of Dad's heartbeat through his freshly pressed button-down shirts and the croon of his voice as he read to me before bedtime. His chin was always prickly after a shave, and I'd push my finger into the dimple at its centre when he came back from the barber.

I float out of my room, still hoping that this is an extension of my dream, that I will wake again to realise it's not happening. The hem of my floral nightdress shakes violently. I stand still, trembling, unable to take in what I see. Our once perfect world is upside down.

My mother stands at an angle, her neck in the forceful crook of my father's left arm, like the innocent person in the movies whose body is being used as a bullet shield. My father holds a knife to her neck. To be more accurate, a sand knife, the one Ba Mailesi uses to prepare thickly buttered bread in the mornings, to cut through chicken thighs and backs as she makes us stew, nshima, and impwa. The sand knife which she so carefully rubs against the dry rock outside the kitchen door to ensure it is sharp enough to slice through bone. Its tip now pierces the soft skin of my mother's neck, drawing a thin line of blood.

Father is crying; mother is crying. Chonta, the neighbour is pleading, her voice shaky but steady – one moment she is begging, the next chastising. Finally, she settles on a convincing tone, the kind you use on a child when you want them to do something for you but are not sure what the power of their own volition will ultimately reveal.

My father is not listening. 'Stella, you are still my wife. Maggie is our only child. You will do as I say and come with me to Nigeria!' His eyes are wild with fury, and without his spectacles, they look unhinged from their sockets. His once smooth chin is a knotted mass of curls. He smells different, like a man who will do anything in this moment. He reeks of desperation.

'Oh, so today I'm your wife? Where have you been, Abs? It's been over a year since we last saw you. Look around; we've moved on! We've survived without you! Kill me if you must! The only person going to Nigeria is you!' my mother spits through clenched teeth.

'Please, Mr Abisola, put the knife down,' Chonta says.

The scene carries on like this for what feels like many hours, but it is probably over in five minutes. Warm lines of urine slide down my thighs, and my nightdress clings to my legs. My eyes tear. My nose burns, and it is moist. I say nothing. I stand there.

Finally, he sinks to his knees. My father releases his weapon, and it clinks on the floor tile. He cries softly into his palms. 'Let's go home, Stella. We are a family.'

*

Weeks in darkness ensue. My existence dwindles to endless days that turn into nights, to faraway voices and whispering shadows. I am being kept 'safe' at homes of family friends. The custody case is in court. Every time they say it, in muted tones, it sounds like a bad disease. Custody. They look at me like I'm the man in my little Bible who Jesus healed from leprosy. Custody doesn't sound so bad to me – in fact, it makes me smile.

I imagine Mum and Dad in a courtroom full of yummy custard, the pair of them before a judge explaining what happened. In my imagination, Dad is leaning back in a chair with his hands steepled while he adjusts his round spectacles with his forefingers. I imagine he is wearing a tie, even though he loathes them and has never owned one. Mum must be perched upright. Her face, brown, and bony, cold and composed like the wooden carving in our living room. Her hands, one over the other, resting against the colourful stripes of her chitenge skirt.

I picture the judge with the face of my Zambian grandfather – Grandpa Charles – big, dark, and round. I have only seen him in photographs and history textbooks.

The judge of my imagination has a curly, white wig like the ones everyone wears in 'My Book of Nursery Rhymes'.

He listens to them while he scoops gooey yellow custard out of a large wooden bowl. He wipes his brow because the air is hot. I know he will understand that grownups fight sometimes, and then he will give them sage advice. He will let them go, and then they can both come and get me. Maybe we can go back to London. Or maybe Mum will say yes, and we can all go to Nigeria. Or maybe Daddy will nod his head and join us here in Lusaka.

Mummy finally comes to pick me up one day in a gleaming white Cressida. She comes right in between the day and the night, when the sky is a mix of watermelon and tangerine, when the sun is about to give way to the moon, when the birds flock and flap their way to their nests.

She's smiling and happy. She glows bright, and I don't know if it's because I haven't seen her in a long time, but she looks golden, like she's been scrubbed and polished and scrubbed again. She looks like an Egyptian goddess. Like an angel. She puts my bag in the back of her new car, and she thanks the people I have been staying with. She says to me, 'Let's go home.'

I agree, even though I don't know any more what that is.

Home is fleeting, beautiful, and fragile. It flutters away like the orange and black butterflies in the garden that I try to catch with my open palms.

After that, I do not see Daddy again. Not for many, many years. My parents' lives continue, each of them finding new lovers and new lives, fresh starts – playing the game of divide and multiply, leaving me in no man's land. A remnant of dreams gone wrong, of pain and despair. A family that will never again be. Or was it ever? Maybe it is all in my imagination.

This I do know, though: it is the beginning, even though it feels like the end.

CHAPTER 2

BUPE KOMBE
LONDON, UK, 1991

ALL THE GROWN-UPS IN my neighbourhood say I came after a storm, which hit us in the middle of a blistering summer. Not the kind of storm with lightning, hail, and snow falling from the sky, but a human one. They say all the nice, regular people they knew flew off the handle. It was like a virus had been put in our water taps. Mrs Croft is always happy to tell the tale in her flat whenever she minds me.

Mrs Croft lives down the street all by herself – well, except for all the ducks in blankets that pad through her living room or when her son comes to visit from Croydon. Her chair rocks back and forth, creaking while she knits more doilies and more tea cosies to make – guess what – more yellow ducks. Her dark house smells like a mishmash of pineapple, gingerbread, and mothballs. She makes me eat coconut peanuts, and the golden caps on her incisors flicker with the movement in the telly whenever she smiles at me. Her eyes glow as she remembers.

'The streets were ablaze with emotions so electric you could feel shocks in the air with your hand! Believe me, Bupe. Jah know! Fire was everywhere. The sounds of shattering glass and alarm bells were deafening. The sirens of fire trucks and ambulances did not stop for three whole days and three whole nights. Police vans were skidding on their backs like overturned beetles, and the kids on the block made bonfires of them!'

I cover my head with a doily but ask her to tell me the story again.

Daddy's version is less dramatic. At times, even disappointing. He says the police were lined up, in all black, moving in a unit, creating turtles with their shields like it was the Roman ages. Bricks hailed on the streets of Brixton like the skies had been opened. Helicopters lit up the alleys like football stadiums in the night, and the shrill sound of sirens remained ringing in their ears long after.

'It was hot, and people were furious!' my father would often tell me. 'Some were terrified, many confused, but your mum was so brave. She was ready to fight for her community, for our home. I begged her to stay, but she melted into the crowd with her fist in the air. So, I came to be with your nan, and we looked after quite a few people who couldn't make it back home.'

What he doesn't say is that Mum was ready to die even with me growing in her belly. She's always ready to die, even while I'm alive and breathing and standing right before her eyes.

Mummy says Daddy proposed to her by the end of that week. She says he did an Una Marson impersonation with an afro wig on his head, because he wanted to make her laugh after she returned home from the riots hurt and sad.

I came into the world months later and they named me Bupe, which means gift in Bemba, my father's language. It is also the middle name of my father's late mother who was Margaret Bupe Kombe. Her portrait sits above the fireplace. She looks young and beautiful, her chin resting on her palm while she smiles upwards and into our living room with perfect teeth 'lined like a healthy cob of maize' as my father says. Mummy says that is the power of dying before you can grow old.

*

My mum's mother lives with us – or rather, we live with her. My nan is my everything. She is Jamaican, and she's the best cook in our borough. She tells me stories about how she worked at my father's friend's home in Marble Arch way back in the sixties, and she shows me the house whenever we pass through to go to the city. The family who owned it were called the Ayomides – also from Africa, but they were from Nigeria. It's a grand house with wide concrete steps that lead to large red doors. The door has brass handles, an astonishingly large lion head knocker, and a fancy mailbox. No one lives in it now. Whenever I see it, it looks empty and alone. Leaves rustle by in swirls and it stands there brooding back at me. Mum and Dad met as teenagers while my nan was working there. Daddy swears it was love at first sight. Mummy says there is no such thing.

Our home has three floors. The ground floor is my favourite because nan made it the most famous curry house in our end, 'Nana West's Curry House'. It's white, green, and yellow. She keeps it so clean and bright that, when I slip and fall, I can see my face looking back at me from the floor. It has black and white portraits of Dr Robert Love, Sam Sharpe, Marcus Garvey, and of course, my nan's secret crush, Alexander Bustamante.

Nana rises every morning at five to begin her preps. The only thing that could stop her from doing this is probably if the world was ending or if her Lord and Saviour, Jesus Christ the Messiah, returned to earth. Every day she gets ready for Him to come down from the heavens.

Mrs Croft says it's not going to be Jesus who returns but His Emperor, Haile Selassie. She says he's coming back to take us all to the Promised Land; says Africans aren't designed to live in Europe, but I don't agree. I love London and I love my street and I love my school and I would never leave. I look at a photograph of the Emperor, his badges gleaming on his dinner coat, hair parted at the left side, waving down into a neat trim. His moustache sits above his lip, and it curls at either side. Is she sure he's coming to get all of us? He looks quite small to me. Mrs Croft alone would take up at least half of his chariot.

The curry house is always warm, making it especially comforting in the winter and festive in the summer. Wafting smells of bell peppers and allspice bring sunshine on the dreariest days. Nan plays calypso all the time, and her favourite is Lord Kitchener. People walk in in a huff, blowing vapour into their gloves, dodging droplets of icy, stinging rain. By the time they leave, Nana says they have fire in their bellies, so they dance their way out, ready to take on London again.

The first floor is our living room. The second is for my nan and me. The top one is for Mum and Dad. Their floor is sometimes dead all day and alive all night. Books are piled everywhere, so high and crooked they look like they will come tumbling down. Some are upright like tents, many closed flat; looking upwards and hoping to be picked next. The windows stay closed and incense sticks fill the air with whatever flavour my mother is advocating for that month. Yes, I know the word 'advocate' because my mum taught it to me before I could say dress or shoes.

Vanilla's her favourite these days. She says it's great for calming tense energy. In my opinion, if that's true, we should throw a vanilla bonfire party for the rest of our lives. When she's not making me paint placards with her or I'm not on someone's shoulders during peaceful protests, I get some slivers of time to have a real mum. When her placards came out her green eyes are sharp and small. She purses her baby pink lips so her mouth looks like it's been sewn from the inside. She dismisses everyone with the wave of her paint stained hands. Maxi Priest plays on blast – unless the issue is more serious, then it's Bob Marley.

Black leggings and turtlenecks hug her curves in every season, and her towering chitenge turban wraps her head. It crowns her olive face all through the day, except for bedtime when she lets her unruly curls loose. Daddy says chitenge is African print cloth that people use in his home country for everything: for slinging babies onto their mothers' backs, for bedding, even for carrying luggage.

Mum's skin is taut and smooth, but her forehead is furrowed with thick lines, especially when she raises her eyebrows to admonish anyone who speaks lowly of themselves. Nana says the lines on her head are from carrying the woes of the world on her shoulders.

*

I have to get permission from my parents to go upstairs ever since I walked in on them kissing in the bathroom. They were completely starkers, and she was on her tiptoes standing on the end of his large leather slippers. The cloudy bathroom didn't smell like incense sticks. It smelt like it does when Mrs Croft's son is in her backyard mucking about with his mates. They shouted for me to knock next time, and I smiled with all my fingers and toes crossed until they ached, hoping that they make a little sister for me.

Some Sundays, Mum and Dad are cooped in their room all day long. Now that I'm older, I've quit waiting on the stairs for them to come out. Instead, I hang out with Nana who's always happy to take me to the High Street if she's not working. She reads me 'My First Book of Bible Stories', but by the time we finish, she's annoyed with me for asking so many questions. Like, how did Mary fall pregnant all by herself? Why hasn't it ever happened to anyone else? Ever? It's hard to believe. And how come Jesus is blond if he came from Jerusalem? Mum says everything began in Egypt and Timbuktu, and that Anglo-Saxons were certainly not roaming the streets of Galilee preaching the gospel in those days. Nana crosses my forehead with anointed oil and prays for me where Mum can't see her do it.

I've always wanted a little sister, but I stopped asking for one when I turned seven. I'm now nine. Nana says I have a cousin on my dad's side who used to live here but now lives in Lusaka (that's all the way in Zambia in Africa) where my dad comes from. Her mum is my dad's little sister, who married Daddy's best friend – Uncle Abisola Ayomide. Daddy does not like to speak about it one bit, but Mum makes him. She says it's not my fault what happened between him and Aunty Stella, so he shouldn't punish me for it.

Mum gave me a picture of my cousin Maggie after I asked nicely. She let me stick it up on my wall. I'm supposed to look after it because it's the only one we have of her. I sit with Maggie sometimes. I pull out my doll's house and set our teacups so we can talk about all the fun stuff we'd do if we were together. I ask her, with my pinkie in the air, 'How was your day today, Cousin Maggie? Did you see any zebra on your way from school?' She stares back at me, wedged between her unsmiling mum and dad, sitting on an ivory couch. They have matching Christmas jumpers. Burgundy and green. I laugh like a grownup. Like Mum does when Dad whispers something in her ear. I slap my thigh and say, 'Maggie, you are so funny. Hilarious you are! Would you like to read something from Enid Blyton with me?' And I read aloud to her, pausing every now and then to ask her how she thinks Felicity and Darrell will do at school this term. 'They're sisters too, you know. I can't wait to meet you. You're the best sister in the whole world'. Nan comes in to switch off my light, and I go to sleep happy.

Dad's lucky. He has one more sibling, my uncle Kabaso, the baby. He pops in every now and then. When he does, Daddy turns into a real worrywart. He fusses over him, making sure he's eaten, got enough pocket money, slept comfortably. I know for a fact that if he could chew his rice and peas for him, he would. They sit up all night playing songs from a long time ago and whispering at the fireplace until it's time for him to leave again.

Every time Uncle Kabaso leaves, Daddy mopes; sad and gloomy, muttering to the grandma in the picture frame. He's so long that he spills out of his old armchair. Everything about my dad is long. His face, his dark eyelashes, his fingers, his toes. He wears a V-necked sweater over everything, and if he takes it off, it's tied around his shoulders.

My mother has one rival for my father's affections: his box of stamps and maps. He handles them with the same concentration Mum has when she's planning a rally. He takes them out of a lockable drawer and lays them in careful order along the coffee table. He examines them with his magnifying glass, bending in low to zoom in, before pulling back for a wider view. He grunts most of the time. Every now and then, he bursts out laughing, rubbing his hands together in glee. He retraces the border of Zambia and his tongue sticks out slightly.

'Do you know that I— we come from Zambia?' he asks.

I nod my head. 'That's where Cousin Maggie is!'

'Yes. Cousin Maggie is there with your aunt Stella. But let's talk about Zambia, OK? It was Northern Rhodesia when I was born.' He pauses, then presses on. 'Your grandfather was instrumental in fighting for independence from Britain. And so was your grandmother because she took care of the family while he faced danger in the name of country. You come from brave blood, I'm afraid'. There is sadness in his eyes.

'Shouldn't that make you proud, Dad?' I grip his index finger.

'Happy?' I scrunch my nose, but he turns his attention back to his map.

'Look at Chinsali.' He hands me the heavy magnifying glass.

'See how far it is from Lusaka, our capital city? It's almost a thousand kilometres away from there, with no electricity, no running water, not much at all – well, except a mission built by the Church of Scotland – and still, it's managed to produce a large stock of freedom fighters. By Jove, it's incredible!'

'Can we go there, Daddy, please?'

He never answers this question. He looks forlorn as he glances at the smiling grandma in the photograph. Instead, he asks me to play 'Tiyende Pamodzi' for him on the old oak piano. It calms him. He sits next to me and his long fingers join mine, so we play in tandem.

Grandmother Margaret smiles on us, and my imagination takes me far away to a land of sunshine and supersized animals hidden in tall golden grass. Freedom fighters whispering secret codes to each other in the heart of the forest, deep inside the belly of the mountains. Fish eagles circling wide open skies, cutting through cotton white tufts of clouds. My heart takes me to a cousin that I so sorely would love to know.

CHAPTER 3

GRANDMOTHER MARGARET CHINSALI, NORTHERN RHODESIA, 1930

THE KOLWE STREAM SNAKED through trees in the knolls to create the spangling northern border of Lubwa Mission. To the south were the teacher and staff houses. The area was dotted with bursts of citrus orchards, bordered by exotic rose bushes. Gay hymns rose from the church when the European missionaries met for administrative meetings.

The football field to the east was quieter now except for the sounds of small children. Most of the men had left in search of work along the new road. Others journeyed farther south to the Copperbelt mines. A fog hung among the trees outside, and the stream gurgled over the hushed sounds of the women in the red brick hut. Margaret's mother lay on the clay floor while a colonial officer in his late teens paced outside.

'There is nothing here for you, officer. I've told you already, my daughter is about to have a baby'. A little African boy carrying the officer's backpack appeared from behind his leg and stepped forward to translate the woman's words to him.

'There are witnesses who say that you have fugitives in your house. You must think I'm stupid. No one is exempt of their hut tax – do you understand?'

'To whom exactly are we paying this hut tax, and why? Is

this land yours to charge its owners a fee? There are no men left to work for you. Leave us in peace.' The translator repeated her words, and the officer stepped up to her. His face in hers.

Their eyes locked – they breathed spittle into each other's faces.

He burst past her into the tiny house and lifted his ill-fitting collar to his mouth. His face morphed, green to purple. Shadows flickered along the walls as midwives surrounded the birthing woman – one kneeling at the head, one bent at the torso, and the last squatting between her quivering thighs. Margaret's mother breathed fast and her face glistened. He looked down at her and strode closer, maintaining eye contact. His oversized boots squeezed air out of them with each step. He looked around the house – a dressing table, chair, stools, and five books stacked next to a domed wooden box. He picked the box up to inspect it. He ran his hands along its intricate casing, and he sniffed it. 'I think I like this. It would make a great gift for the district commissioner. I don't think you'll need it since you'll be in prison, and quite frankly, I need a promotion.'

The birthing woman on the dirt floor spat in between her grunts.

The previously kneeling women stood upright. Hot calabashes hissed in the nooks of their arms. They advanced towards him.

He spun out of the room and gave a warning. 'I'll – I'll let you go this time. But if I get another report, I'll send you somewhere so far away, you will never ever set foot on this soil again!'

The room fell silent. It grew dark once the curtains at its entrance closed. The baby was left to be born in peace. Ululation erupted from the women. The baby girl was cleaned and oiled – wrapped in fine cloth made of soft tree bark called ichilundu. She was named a gift from the ancestors. The precious wooden box was carefully emptied. A set of shiny beads was placed around her waist. Protection and fertility would be her portion.

Later, when the red rimmed sun had dropped low enough to hide behind the forest and its lulling stream, the mother was moved from her birthing place. The reed mat that was left was peeled away carefully.

A row of uneven wooden board chips revealed a trapdoor. It opened wide. Three men lay straight as logs in a mass grave. The ladies held their breath while the little baby suckled her mother's bosom. Suddenly, she stopped. And there was silence. She wriggled and whined until she howled into the evening. The three men sprang to life gulping and huffing to draw in deep, deep breaths.

They were fed porridge from a battered iron pot. It was scoffed down.

'It is a longer journey, but if you want to avoid the officers, go westwards, against the current of the river. After two days, you will find our colleagues at the Chipoma Falls. You can trust them. Tell them that you are going to Abercorn. From there, you can cross the lake at Tanganyika. They will see you through to safety.'

They thanked their hosts and rained incantations on the new baby.

And that is how Margaret Bupe Kombe came into the world.

CHAPTER 4

MAGGIE OLUWASEUN AYOMIDE
LUSAKA, ZAMBIA, 1991

GOING UP INTO THE air, weightless and fluid, I break into smaller bits, and I can see everything – I am happy and free. I see children in my schoolyard running and playing in the dust of Kabwata in green and yellow uniforms, patterned heads of cotton braids glistening with pomade. A view of our home in London – cold Christmases and rainy walks to school, my father and me under my toddler-sized umbrella, him humming to the tune of 'Rain Rain Go Away', the steam from hot steak and kidney pies in tinfoil, the warmth of my earmuffs, ice skating with my mother – of me in my clown suit on red-nose day, of my parents holding each of my hands to lift me over a puddle as we cross the street.

My father reappears, his eyes rolling backwards, flashing a knife in his right hand. He drops it and begins to cry.

My alarm clock screeches at my bedside. The morning rush begins. At school, I get to meet her officially – Mother Zambia. She is shown to me on the smooth surface of a cold map. She looks like a curled up baby in the belly of a proud standing woman, the one they have told me is Africa.

'We are a randrocked country!' my bony teacher emphasises. Her tongue – no respecter of the letters 'l' or 'r'. Her towering afro, jet black and glycerine filled, creates its own shadow against the chalkboard. Her turquoise polyester skirt sits high on her waist, secured by a metal butterfly on an elastic belt. The butterfly looks like it could flutter away, and her skirt, if unravelled, would be followed by consonants and vowels tumbling out from behind her, waiting to be taught to us – pleat by pleat.

'Gleen is the colour of our rand, our vast natural resources'. Her arms are held open, her chin is bobbing, and her wide eyes are twinkling, looking out to an imaginary horizon. Her hands are white with chalk dust up to her wrists.

'Olange lepresents our wealth in minerals, copper especiary. Do you know we are the second rah-gest producer of copper on this entire grobe? Second only to Chile in South America?'

'Leddy! Is for the brahd we shed – fighting for independence!' She holds our attention with the fervour of her speech. 'And brrack' – now enthused, we wait on her theatrical pause, like she's about to break into song – 'lepresents the colour Of Our Skin.' We gasp.

Some kids waggle their heads in disbelief. Others clap.

Three students are being punished. They are on their knees with their hands straight up in the air at the front of her desk. They quake, both from fatigue but also from holding in the laughter stuck in their tummies. The school bell finally rings, and everyone collects their beaten brown bookcases and teddy bear shaped toy drinks from the back of the classroom. I grab my fuchsia nylon bag and head to the pickup zone.

Later at home, as I lie in the bath, I ponder what she said to us. Why haven't I seen anyone with black skin my whole life? Maybe Mrs Moyo doesn't know brown is not black? Surely no one is black – everyone is some shade of brown. My friend Aisha is half Indian with long curly hair down to her waist, and her grandmother is Chewa from Eastern Province. Is she black too? Or is she not?

The rhythmic dap-dap of rope against tar and the clapping hands of little girls creeps out of the hidden corners of my mind. It takes me back to when I first heard of this strange phenomenon.

My last autumn in London – red, ginger, and auburn leaves floated all around my patent black school shoes. Me, standing isolated, chin on my chest, in the naughty corner with an N sticker on my grey pinafore. The sounds of children's laughter and shrieks from the thrill of games of tag at playtime in the schoolyard. Not being allowed to join them because I was forbidden from doing so – not to be spoken to, and to speak to no one. The sniggering sounds and incessant teasing from the two girls who had refused to let me join in on their skip rope game two days prior.

'We don't play with black girls,' they said. The one with the curly blond hair spat on the ground. They joined hands and walked away – a duo, still short a third person to make their game work. For the first time, I walked the park, desperately searching every face for this colour – no one else was 'black', except for a few boys who already played with the seniors. Dejected and alone, I played over her words in my head as I looked around me.

Black? What did she mean?

At home, when I joined my father in the living room, I turned his hand over and over again. I stroked his palm for some time and looked at him seriously.

'What is it, my darling?'

'Dad, your hand has two colours.'

'What do you mean?'

I turned it upwards and stroked his palm. 'Your hand on the inside is pink. Does that make you white?' I turned it over. 'Or are you a black too?'

He laughed and said that we are in fact black, but colour is not what is on your skin – it is what is in your heart. 'Come to think of it,' he said, stroking my head tenderly, 'I think you're more toffee!' He tickled me until I forgot the question.

At assembly the following morning, Mr Holiday strummed his guitar for his miniature audience. He announced that he would like to see me in his office.

'Margaret Ayomide, Melissa and Sandy say you approached them in the playground, snatched their skipping rope, and said a terrible word to them! They say you called them stupid. I'm afraid I will have to give you the naughty sign for the rest of the week. No playtime allowed until then.'

'I didn't say anything like that to them, Mr Holiday! I've never ever said that word!' My head shook in my disbelief.

'I'm disappointed in you, young lady. Lying will give you an extra day in the naughty corner'.

He wielded his pen like a little wand, and he dismissed me. 'Run along now', he mumbled.

If that was what black was, why would we put it on our country's flag? Is black a good thing or a bad thing? At least here, whether it's good or bad, I don't feel different because of the colour of my skin. I feel different in other ways.

Mrs Moyo says I should say 'loolabee', but I still say 'lullaby'. When she calls my last name, it's the only one that starts with an A and sounds like it does. The teachers in the staff room turn to inspect me whenever I go there to ask a question. 'This name, it's foreign?' they ask while they cluck their tongues and sip their tea. 'Yes, but my mother comes from here.' They nod their heads slowly.

I wish, for once, I wouldn't be singled out.

*

I am full of questions lately. It irritates my mother because she prefers silence. But sometimes she indulges me, like when I want to know how she met my dad.

Over slow cooking pots of pig feet, jollof rice, and chibwabwa, she tells me how she came to meet him – again. She, beautiful and young, was the daughter of a revered but beleaguered freedom fighter, the second of three children, smart and hardworking, at university in London. He was the son of a Nigerian commodities trader and had a migrant mother from Jamaica.

'London was cold and isolating sometimes. Even with all the people in the world there, one could feel all alone.'

'So how did you meet Daddy?'

'I was getting ready to host some friends of mine from my politics class. I was looking forward to a mean bowl of beef stroganoff and a game of Scrabble after. I kept pulling back the sleeve of my coat to check my watch because I knew I was late, and I didn't want my friends milling about my flat in the cold. The shopping bags I got were so heavy, I asked the stingy lady at the till if she could double bag and she said no. In a rush, I left the shop and the wind was sharp against my skin.'

'And then what, Mummy?'

'Patience, young one. Let the story come, I always tell you.' She wipes the wooden kitchen counter with a damp cloth and rubs her hands with soapy water. She lifts the lid of a steel pot and it blows out steam. She stirs it gently. It has pig feet boiling in a stew. Peppery aromas flavour the small kitchen. Flies outside buzz against the net of the window in a futile attempt to partake in our supper.

'I was walking against the wind with my head bent into my coat. In a panic about the time, I broke into a slight jog.' She laughs. 'And in a flash, my bags were not heavy anymore! I watched all the contents scatter all over the icy pavement.

'A tub of strawberry yoghurt splashed all over my shoes. I was so upset. I jumped high enough to lift my knees into the air. I punched my fists in all directions, and I screamed in frustration. Your dad came my way nearly skidding over a rolling can of baked beans. He picked it up, and I shouted at him. I told him to mind his own business and not to touch other people's messes. It was my mess!'

'Mummy!' I'm laughing. 'You just like to fight with people. How can you keep a mess to yourself?'

'Well, he bent down to scoop the items up while I screeched.

His hair was a mass of wet, sticky looking Jheri curls, and he wore dark glasses in the bleak weather. His trousers looked like they would split open if he bent down any further. I wasn't impressed. But then he insisted on finishing cleaning up, and before I knew it, he was done. He stood up to look at me. It was the craziest thing ever! I remembered him from my days as a teenager because he was friends with your uncle CJ.'

'And then?'

'And then, Maggie Ayomide, he smiled warmly on a freezing day and offered to carry my groceries all the way to my apartment. He stayed that night and joined us for dinner. Him and I scooped the Scrabble trophy and my friends kept asking me where I found him.'

I set the marble laminated table for two; Mum at the head and me to her right. I struggle to fill up our cups of water while the ice blocks in the plastic jug clink against each other. She plays Diana Ross and Marvin Gaye's 'You're a Part of Me' on the record player. I sway to the music, and I see them in my mind. The two of them talking late into the night, eating soy dipped dim sums at the local Chinese restaurant, head to head beneath neon lights. The pair dancing out of disco house parties in swinging bellbottoms and polyester button downs, just like in the pictures we had in London. I see both of them in love and happy. I wish we could go back there and start all over again. She's dancing her way to the table. I say a prayer in my heart. 'Dear God, I promise to go to Lagos and find my father no matter what happens. I will be a good girl, and I will study hard so both Mum and Dad will be proud of me. That way, one day when I find him, they will remember that I belong to the both of them, and then I can set the dining table for three'.

CHAPTER 5

BUPE KOMBE
LONDON, UK, 1991

MUM DROPS ME OFF at school in a rush, but she only leaves after she's questioned my teacher about our meals and double checked that I get the vegetarian portion with no artificial ingredients, no MSG, no anything really – it's her latest cause. She says modern food in the West is killing our people with 'obesity and all manners of cancer!'

She points it out all the time now, like when we saw a blubberous lady (Mum says its rude to use that word) who couldn't get off the bus unassisted, huffing at the driver to get her walking stick, sweating from the work of standing up from her seat and being heaved onto the pavement. All the teenage boys jeered, but Mum told them to put a sock in it, and they grew sullen like scolded puppies. Thankfully, nan keeps a secret plate of greasy, falling-off-the-bone oxtail and some roti for me after the shop is closed. She pulls it out when the door on the top floor is sealed shut and muted whispers are all we hear for the night.

I hang my bag along a row of hooks on the wall, beneath the mural of art done by the Year 4s from last year. I get lost in their strokes – the colours light up like shots of neon in my brain as though I orchestrated them while they worked. I hover in the walkway, mesmerised by th–Pop! Bang! Thunk! I'm smashed to the ground with the weight of some idiot who's blasted into the room. Jerome Simmons lands on top of me in a heap. I'm so mad I shout at him, but he shouts back. Before we know it, we are in trouble, and we have to be the first to participate in the class exercise for the morning.

Jerome. He's always late or early. He's always happy or sad, no in betweens. He wears a leather hat on his head, and his mother insists on Rasta prints for his coat. He's got a tall table cut with a karate kid ponytail that's planted on the back of his head. Of course, the hat comes off once class starts, but its back on as soon as he's on his way home. He annoys me, but there is something about him that keeps my eyes glued to his face.

It's Careers Day, and we've been sent to the clothes room to do a make believe of what we'd like to be when we grow up. Our punishment is to help each other find something suitable. I look at the outfits, and I simply cannot choose one. I like the idea of a firefighter, but then I don't like the idea of being burnt. I hate the idea of being a doctor, because I don't like sick people. They always look filmy and grey. I grab an artist's apron, a crown for my head, long silk gloves, and a pair of soldier's boots. There is no outfit for a placard painter.

Jerome leans with his back against the wall, supported by his foot.

'This stuff's all whack. Like, I don't know what we're even doing here.' After a few minutes, he's pointing at my outfit, laughing with his mouth wide open until our teacher calls for us to hurry up and join the rest of the kids. He finally settles on a police jacket and hat. He bends to tie his shoelaces, and a string dangles from under his shirt. It flashes a battered tin key.

'What's that for?' I ask him.

'Mind your own business.'

'I'll tell on you if you don't tell me.'

'Shush! It's my key for when I get home, OK? Not everyone is lucky enough to have a mum and a dad and a nan who run your own family restaurant, you know!'

He sucks his teeth and skulks away.

After school, I watch him go. He walks on his own, and I imagine him going home to an empty flat, making himself cornflakes with lumpy milk from last week or warming leftovers in the microwave.

*

The next day when school's done, he strolls over to me at the bench outside. My mum is late, and when she is, I sometimes take the bus with Mrs Croft, who should be here any minute now. Jerome, he's not your everyday face, I wouldn't say. His face kinda has to grow on you. He looks like he could use some moisturiser and a comb. He's shaped like a square. Wide jaws, wide shoulders, boxy eyes. Skin dark as midnight, and a bottom lip that shines pink. He looks like he's been jostled in a fight.

'Can I join you?' He's speaking to me, but he's looking elsewhere like he's distracted. His black bag hangs off one shoulder. I turn my head both ways to check that it is me he wants to sit with.

I nod.

I try to open my mouth, to let my voice out, but my brain won't give me anything to say. Instead, he begins the conversation, still looking away from me.

'I can't stand it, you know.'

'Stand what?' I manage to ask.

'The African kids. They think they're the kings of the black race. Especially the Nigerians.'

'Wot do you mean? If they're not, who is?'

'Us, Jamaicans'. He flexes his muscles and lays a fist on his chest.

'Really? Aren't we all the same?'

'Swear down we ain't!' He snaps his index finger against his middle and thumb, which are pressed together.

'Why on earth not?' I feel my face grow hot.

'Ask them.' He points at older guys down the street.

We watch them through the bars of the fence. They look trendy, and their hair is styled with angular lines and curls. Some are tall and hefty, laughing in the air, leaning on a tiny old car, boom boxes on shoulders. One group is clad in gold jewellery, blasting dancehall, the other is playing African rhumba, and the girls they're with are shaking their hips to it. I squint my eyes in case I'm missing something.

'I can't see what you mean.' I feel daft. I wish I was more with it; like him.

'You wouldn't see it, would you? You're such a square.'

I reel at his choice of words.

'I'm African and Jamaican, so no, I don't agree with you. What I do know though, is that if what you say is true, it should make me a queen then, innit?' I'm smiling, smug now. I win.

He shrugs, and he eyes my secret stash. I offer him a Jamaican patty from my nan. He gobbles it down, his jaws clanging like he's made of tin.

'Here's an example. You eat plantain, yeah? My mate Femi and I just had a fight because he says we're supposed to say plahn-*teyn*, and I say that's wrong. It's plan-ten. They can't come in here and tell us how to pronounce our own food.'

He faces his full body my way. 'What do you say? Whose side are you on?' My brain fails me again. I stutter back a cloud of vapour into the cold air.

'Have you ever been to Africa?' he says, smacking his lips in between mouthfuls.

'No. But I would love to go. I have a cousin there!' My eyes grow big, and my shoulders slouch.

'But … my dad says it's not safe there. My grandad was taken away because he said something that the government didn't like.'

'Geez, that's cold. I'm sorry. Do you know what he said to tick them off?'

I shake my head. 'Thanks. It's not like I've met him, so it kinda doesn't hurt.' I try to look cool and relaxed, like him. But my body falls into an awkward slanted position instead. I will my mouth to let out something decent.

'Have. You. Been … to Jamaica?' The words sputter out like a nearly empty bottle of ketchup being squeezed.

'Never. My mum's been saving up for it since I was little. Every year I watch her work and work 'til she's too tired to talk to me when she gets home. No lie, I gave up on that dream ages ago. I wish she would too. She was gutted when she couldn't make it for her sister's wedding last Christmas.' He looks at his sneakers and rubs his hands against each other in slow circles.

Mrs Croft hobbles our way in a woollen hat and summons for me with a wave.

'So, Jerome Simmons, that should make us both from London then, innit?'

He grabs my hand and holds onto it. His hand is rough and bumpy, but it's warm. It makes me feel like I finally have a real friend. One I can talk to. One who can talk back. One who can see the inside of me. The playground lights up as the sun shows itself from behind a bed of clouds.

'I suppose so. That should make us Londoners.'

He looks at me and smiles, shouting as I leave, 'Maybe, Miz Bupe, it makes you de Queen of de Sarrf.'

CHAPTER 6

MAGGIE OLUWASEUN AYOMIDE
LUSAKA, ZAMBIA, 1991

ZAMBIA IS FULL OF secrets and mysteries. Adults appear as shadows in the dead of night. The keyhole in our corridor allows me to see things. It is amazing how such a tiny lightbulb-shaped indentation in a door can reveal so much to one on the other side. It keeps me concealed – I am addicted to watching them. My heart is pumping. My throat is dry. I have not put much thought to what should happen if I am caught.

Through it, I see movement. Beers. Clouds of smoke. Papers scattered everywhere. The offensive smell of cigarettes seeps through the slits of my door so I pinch my nose. The sound of fingers beavering at a typewriter and the ping each time a new sentence is begun. Rhumba melodies of Franco play on low volume. I watch them. I hear them. They repeat 'The hour has come', making one o'clock signs with their index fingers pointing upwards to the sky, thumbs bent slightly to the right. In broad daylight, when there is no door to hide me, they make a V with their fingers and shout, 'V for Victory!'

In the afternoons, once it has rained, the smell of wet soil mixed with the bitter smell of squashed flying ants calls all of us – the children who live in the flats named after the parastatal companies they are owned by, like ZESCO, BOZ, INDECO – we all come out to play, and we identify each other by our respective acronyms. Finally, free to be outside, we take turns at each other's yards. I am a ZESCO kid. The boys bring their best wire cars, some even have wire passengers in them: mums and dads with a child in the back seat. We show off our Thumbelina chairs made carefully from stalks of greenish brown grass.

We draw in the damp sand with sticks and create a map for a game called 'Touch'. While we do this, we sing the words of the cartoon advert that comes on every day. Our skirts tucked into the sides of our panties so we can jump and dance, mouths blue from mulberries we've picked along the fence. We dance like Tshala Muana turning our wrists in circles while we chant:

> Keep the flame burning, do the right thing,
> The future's in our hands—TIYENDE PAMODZI—
> Let us work together every day, Vote
> for UNIP and KK… and Zambia, the
> promised land.

Ba Mailesi yells out to me from the car park. I shove my flipflops on so that we can buy some food for tomorrow. At the shops, the shelves don't have anything you can eat. No bread, no sugar, no sausages, no drinks, not even mealie-meal – just rows and rows of washing powder staring back at us. So, we walk further up the road where we linger in a queue under the scorching sun to buy bread and eggs. People in the back crane their necks to get a view of the front. Murmurs of shorter queues at other stores pass through the line in waves, but everyone remains stuck, like their feet are planted in mud.

When we finally make it into the shop, it is hotter than outside – and dark. Only one more person is in front of us, an elderly lady whose back is as bent as a fishing hook.

'Four loaves please'.

'One customer, one loaf, madam. You know the rules.'

'Please, sir, I'm begging you. I have five orphans and six children in my house. One loaf will not get us through this evening.'

'Next!' the man calls. The room falls silent as everyone scrutinises the scene. Slit eyes glower in the dark stuffy store. People's gazes swing from loaf of bread to shop owner, shop owner to old lady. We hear the shuffling of shoes against the floor. The elderly lady holds the shopkeeper's eye until his head bows down to his chest. He sets his stare on the loaf that remains stationary on the counter. Untouched.

A shrill scream pierces the dense air. 'You will kill us! Twafwa! Please, I'm begging you.'

'There is nothing I can do, madam. I advise you to take this one here and join another queue at the next shop. My hands are tied.'

The long line of customers morphs into a pulsating crowd, pushing forwards and pulling backwards. Hunger and anger meet. Harsh sounds escape customers' mouths in quiet bursts. Heavy words I do not understand fully, fly around the room. I am squashed in the heat of moist bodies. Unfamiliar fabrics brush against my face. My heart races. The whiffs of sweet dough and sweat engulf me.

The old woman unwraps the knot of her chitenge which sits high at her waist, and she bends to wipe her brow. Her shoulders shake fiercely until she disappears into the street with a single loaf tucked under her arm. While Ba Mailesi buys our goods, the old lady reappears, and she puts a crooked finger to her lips. She summons me with her free hand. I sneak out of the dark shop to see what the lady wants to say.

'Your grandmother wants you to know something. She says for you to look for the wooden box. You will find the answers in it.'

'What box?' I ask. 'And which grandmother?' The lady shuffles away back into the crowds, and this time she does not return. 'Which grandmother?' I cry. Ba Mailesi comes to smack me on the back of my head for leaving her without saying anything. 'Let's hurry home before it gets dark.'

I feel sorry for the shop owner because we leave him shifting from foot to foot while an angry throng of people look like they will climb over his wooden counter. The whole way home, the lady's words bounce around in my head.

*

Today, I am lucky enough to shop with Mum at the duty free store on Cairo Road. It is well lit and has blasting air conditioner and cold fridges. It is stocked with things I saw only in London. Here we get apples, soft drinks, Quality Street, Weetabix, and cornflakes. There's even music to make your day nicer as you walk the aisles. People stop to greet us in the shop, gentlemen take off their hats and hold them to their chest while they speak to my mother in low whispers using big words like liberation and de-mo-cra-cy.

Other adults walk away from Mum, even when she greets them warmly. They make sure that their children do not wave back at me either, and they sweep them away from us, like mother hens do their chicks. I look at Mum, but she clenches her fists and snaps at me when I ask her why they don't wave back. She focuses on the shopping list, examining the handwritten prices on the goods. I want to stroke her bony arm and tell her it's OK. We don't need those people – we have each other.

At the till, her hands shake while she counts the pound notes in her purse. She looks around and she locks eyes with a stout, bow legged man at the door. She gives a soft nod, but his eyes remain watchful. Later she tells me that his job is to monitor who has foreign notes on them and why. I wish I could bring Dad back, so maybe he could take us to London, and she wouldn't have to worry about buying apples in this expensive store where people watch the money in your purse.

At the exit, the man blocks our way with his full body. Mum grips me firmly but she says nothing. After moments, she hands a receipt to him. He pores over it. Up and down, up and down, until he steps aside, releasing us into the world.

We jump into her car, and we sit in silence for a while before she twists the dial on the radio to hear the lunchtime news. I look outside my window, too bruised to hide the tears threatening to fall down my face. She rubs my arm. She raises my chin in the crook of her finger, turning my face back in her direction and says, 'Don't be sad, Maggie'.

I sniff and wipe my nose with my free sleeve.

'Be proud, my daughter. One day, I promise, your grandfather will come back home, and people will run in your direction to greet you – heartily. Integrity is the only thing in this world that will create second chances for you. Things will change soon. It can't stay this way forever.' I don't understand what she's saying, but I can see that she wants me to be happy, so I nod.

She offers me a bar of chocolate, and I open it roughly. It is so rich, so sweet, that it fills every bit of my mouth, and I chew in sticky circles. It tastes so foreign now. I close my eyes to make sure that the feeling pastes itself to my memory because I don't know when I'll have one again. Voices on the radio talk about 'elections' and 'voting'. It makes her turn back towards me with a wide smile. 'I know! Let's do something nice together. Let's go get our hair done!' The car shakes as she turns the engine on.

We drive up the road to Moye's, a salon with colourful triangles and patterns at its window. Inside, the lady combs out my hair. It expands wider and wider until she exclaims, 'Owe! Like Moses and the burning bush! This is a lot of hair coming out of nowhere!' The room rises with laughter.

'But don't worry – I have some magic tricks.' She places an iron comb on heat, and the lady begins to tame my thicket.

Afterwards, they braid it in mesh-patterned cornrows going from the right side of my head all the way to the left. The sulphuric smell of a candle flame to mesh creeps into my nose as they burn the ends of my synthetic braids.

The lady rubs the melted ends of my braids to make a permanent stop for my beads. She does it like her fingers are indestructible. Mum comes out of the large drier and they take out her huge rollers: yellow and green in front, and dark blue and red at her nape. We return home and play I Spy, and I think I've won the game because she says I can stay up late today.

Aunty Chonta from next door bustles through the back door in the evening. She comes bearing gifts: a few blue cans of Ohlsson's Lager for her and Mother. Her shoulder pads are so large, they look like she is about to fly away. Her eye shadow is bright, her hair a mass of curls. On the balcony, she faces the moon and stars, as though she has plans to go off into space. In whispers, she bickers about the rations, expanding queues for sugar, riots – and finally the curfew. She holds my mother's hand and gives her big pleading eyes, 'Mwana Kombe, do something, please! We are relying on you like your father before you.'

'I know, my sister. We are working hard behind the scenes. The power is now in our hands. With that vote, we are all responsible for this country. We have to do it together. Tell everyone you know to cast that ballot when the time comes.'

*

My mother and I settle into our new routine, and soon things begin to feel normal. Whenever she is home, we work around each other – when she is playing her records and moving things in the living room, I am quiet in my bedroom. When she is in her bedroom, I creep out to watch 'Fat Albert', and on Saturdays, 'it's The Beam'. Bobby Brown sings about needing a girlfriend, and I can't wait to be a teenager so I can be out every night like the aunty next door with the large shoulder pads.

From our balcony, I watch all the dads come home in Peugeots – cars with angry faces and big, round eyes. The kids leap for joy along the driveway. The mums are in the passenger side, wearing floral dresses with belts at the waist and hair set in curls. Their lips are painted rouge, and they scurry into the flats to make meals whose aromas float upstairs to our own. The children open their dads' car doors asking what bounty they have returned with. Some boys sit on their fathers' laps and steer the wheel, pretending that they are all grown up. They collect handbags and brief cases as they give a report of what happened at school that day.

Before bedtime, Ba Mailesi soaks me in a strong Dettol solution with a waxy bar of soap. She scours me until my skin is raw. She dresses me in polyester pyjamas that stick to my skin. In the dark, my pyjamas spark green and blue whenever I move, and it is terribly hot. Mosquitoes buzz inside my ears.

I shut my eyes to smile at Dad. I let him twirl me in the air and kiss me on my cheek. He lets me carry his briefcase into the flat, and once he's sat down, I take off his shoes for him. I sit at his feet, and I look at his smiling face. He calls for Mum, and she comes out with a tray full of glistening roasts. She sets them on a table with shiny sweets. She's wearing an apron with pretty frills at the edges, and her hair is flowing. I recite my times table for Dad, and he is so impressed with me, he claps and laughs.

'Come and see this child of mine!' he yells. 'Come and see my Maggie! She is so smart! She is just like me'.

When a hooter outside jolts me back to reality, a sunken ceiling board glares back at me through the dim light. I close my eyes again, but Dad is no longer there. He has gone. I can't smell him. I can't see him. I can't hear him. I squeeze my eyes tighter to search for him, but instead, all I find is a box. A delicately carved wooden box which domes at the top like a pyramid.

A voice prods me towards her room. A woman's voice. It doesn't sound very clear, but I do hear her call my name. I feel a gravitational pull towards the pyramid box that Mum keeps at the top of her wardrobe. It's like I can see a lady in a shimmering dress holding it and calling me to her. Mrs Moyo would say it is the devil at work because I cannot help myself. The box. It is often left on the floor or under her bed on the mornings when Mum has cried herself to sleep at night.

I push the stool from her dressing table, which has noticeably fewer perfumes than when she was still with Dad. Her jewellery has now simplified to copper and forest green malachite. I wonder where she put all the diamonds and rubies she used to wear in London?

I climb onto the mauve velvet seat and stretch to reach the mysterious box. The stool rocks, as one of its legs is slightly shorter than the rest. I balance myself and listen for Ba Mailesi. She is snoring away on the mattress in my room.

I pull the box out slowly, and it succumbs to my tiny hands. I step back down and get comfortable beneath Mum's three quarter sized bed while the fan in the ceiling makes creaking sounds from all its hard labour. Newspaper clippings with headlines jump out into the room and dance around me in circles.

'Wall Street's Blackest Hours … Stocks Plunge 508 Points'
'Minister Loses Wife to Watery Accident'
'Kombe Arrested for Treason'

There are photographs of a little girl and her parents. The girl – she must be my cousin Bupe. I've only ever heard of her from my dad when we were in London. She's the only cousin I have, so it has to be her. She makes funny faces in most of her pictures. Her cock eyes cross like they've been pulled by a string in opposite directions, and her tongue dangles like she's been strangled. In one of them, she's smiling with her parents behind her. In another, she's with my Uncle Kabaso. His picture makes me throw it back down. He wears his hair long. Aunt Jasmine has the words 'Lionheart Gal' spread across her chest, and she wears a huge chitenge turban on her head. All of them pose at what looks like a museum with faces of famous people like Michael Jackson. The box is filled with letters from Uncle CJ begging her to let us meet, to take me to London to see my cousin. I want to kiss them and hold them and call them. Now, not tomorrow. My hands shake as I wonder why Mum keeps all these things to herself. I remember that there was something else I saw here.

I shuffle the papers to go back to the headline about the watery accident.

The door bursts open.

Whack! My mother strikes me across my face with a mighty slap. She gets on all fours to collect her scattered papers and photographs while her chest heaves heavily.

'How could you? Why would you?' she spits. She is uncontrollably upset, and she stuffs the papers back into the box.

I do not have the strength to say anything. I'm strewn along the floor. A ringing in my ears sounds as loud as an alarm bell. The sting across my cheek feels visible. I touch it, and it stings.

'Go to your room. Now!' Ba Mailesi appears at the door, as terrified as me. She leads me to my room, and we sit in silence while I cry in the dark.

Later, into the wee hours of the morning, I creep back out at the sound of Mum's sobs. She swirls blocks of ice in a glass of whiskey. There is loud thunder rumbling outside, and the rain pours like when Noah warned the people. Her curtains billow wide. They are sucked back into the mesh of the windows and flap repeatedly. Lightning follows and the room's light flickers for a second.

*

I sit down on the floor, inside her room, at the entrance of her bedroom door. She picks up a large pair of scissors, and she begins to cut her hair right down to her skin. Long wafts of it fall slowly to the ground until they make a soft woolly mess on her floor. A steady buzz fills the small room as she turns on Daddy's old clippers. She takes the machine to her head and lets its spiky edge do its work. Round and round, smoothly, until there was nothing left at all. A rough mound of skin on a raw, grey head is what is left. She doesn't look golden and shiny anymore. She looks like the earth. Like a barren anthill made of clay. It makes me cry.

'Don't you ever go through my things again. Do you understand?' She's speaking to me through the reflection in the mirror. Her voice is calm now. Steady.

'Yes, Mum.'

'Good. Now, go to sleep.'

I continue to watch her for a moment more. As though what has happened tonight isn't enough trouble for one day, I ask her, 'Where is my grandmother? What happened to her?'

'She died.'

'How?'

'She had an accident, Maggie.'

'What was she like?'

'She was graceful and elegant. She spoke the most poetic Bemba you've ever heard. She was caring and selfless.'

'Why don't we have pictures of her?'

She shrugs and takes a moment before she answers. 'I'll put some up tomorrow, OK? Now, go to bed. It's late. And forget about everything you saw today. That is all in the past.'

CHAPTER 7

GRANDMOTHER MARGARET
COPPERBELT, NORTHERN RHODESIA, 1949

CECIL RHODES AVENUE IN Ndola rolled out before Margaret like a dream. It gleamed with endless rows of pastel coloured motor cars. European ladies strapped chin high in chesro frocks and rouge on their cheeks. Their dogs walked beside them in collars. One or two had African women in patterned uniforms carrying their children about five paces behind. The smell of baked cakes and hot teas filled the promenade. There were no trees or hills. Open skies showed off tall buildings that shimmered in the sun. Little newspaper boys donned miniature suits and bowling hats calling out for buyers.

*

Margaret set her bag down, right next to her sewing machine. She dusted her skirt briskly and coughed as she was haloed in a cloud of red dust. Two days on the back of an open lorry had seen her come from Chinsali. The sand in her mouth and eyes would never fully come out, she thought. The urge to say hello to someone came naturally, but it suddenly struck her that she knew no one here. The people all walked and talked so fast. She began to palpitate. Had she made a mistake to come here? Would Charles send her back home for coming without his permission? She dug into her purse and pulled out the letter from Charles that she, herself had painstakingly prepared. After much practice, it was a close enough imitation of his handwriting. It was a miracle that none of the police checks had sent her back. She looked at the address in the top corner.

An African man who was calling for passengers to fill his small lorry ran up to her. 'Do you need transport, madam?'

'Yes, please,' She hesitated before she handed him the paper.

'Can you take me to this place?' He scratched his head.

'Do you have your pass? I don't want trouble. Kitwe is not far from here, but it's not that close either.' She nodded before she fumbled through her purse to give him coins.

'Oh, upfront payment? The sun is shining on Me today. Let's go!'

*

The man dropped her off at the busy mouth of a vast compound of corrugated iron roofs. They waved in melting mirages into brick huts that shot out of sooty soil. The houses were tightly packed rows of thousands of steel shacks. Shirts and skirts hung out to dry on hibiscus shrubs, and windowsills.

A group of women laughed together under the shade of a mango tree.

'Excuse me. I'm looking for the home of Charles Kombe, please.'

One grazed her bottom teeth along the white of a mango seed, the other smoked a cigarette, and the last one was barefoot. Their faces, however, were identically painted in a talcum of some kind and charcoal darkened their brows. Margaret held on tight to her bag. Her other arm twitched with the weight of the sewing machine.

'What section is he in?'

'Urhm Section B, please. House number 43.'

'You're Bemba, eh?'

'Yes. And you?'

'We call ourselves the NR trio. She's Tonga, I'm Lozi, and our friend here is Chewa.'

'Do you speak to each other in English then?'

They laughed. 'Of course, we do. This is the city after all. Come, we will show you to his house. We've heard about him and his speeches from everyone who goes to the teachers' union meetings. He speaks well – with fire in his belly. Is he a– relative of yours?'

She chose to ignore this. 'Show me the way, please.'

The four of them waved through masses of houses and people. Broods of hens criss-crossed the narrow paths while bleating goats drank from bathwater that tunnelled through the rows of houses.

Margaret stood at the veranda for a few minutes and sat her sewing machine on the bright red concrete. Spiky aloe vera curled out of old, peeling tins on either side of the entrance. A black bicycle leaned against the wall, its basket and elastic rope still intact. Margaret could feel the NR trio's eyes on her back. Her hands shook. Her neck burned. Her feet throbbed. She patted her face with a handkerchief, and finally, she knocked on the tiny door.

'Who's there—' The door opened a crack. It banged shut for ten seconds before he opened it again.

'Margaret! What are you doing here?'

'I've come home. To be with my husband.'

She looked inside the musty house. Behind him lay colourful bundles of cloth – women's clothes heaped up on a chair, unsightly balls of fabric lined along the floor. Margaret's jaw set. She turned to look at him.

'She must be an untidy lady to leave all her things like this. She doesn't have an iron?'

'What? Oh, you mean the clothes? Ah, my love,' he looked embarrassed, 'That is for my business. I buy second hand clothes from the Mokambo border at the Congo, and I sell them here.'

Margaret's heart sunk.

'You sell women's clothes?' She took a step further into the small house and touched a dress. She unbundled it, stroked it – inspecting its buttons. She let the tips of her fingers follow the stitches in its hem.

'And you have time to choose all these dresses?'

'I have a contact on the other side. Her name is Fabiola Manuel. She makes the selections and has them ready for me. I sell them here. This compound alone has more than 10,000 people all looking for something nice to wear.'

She looked at the floor, fiddling her thumbs.

His voice fell. 'That's what I use to send money to you for the farm. My teacher's salary cannot sustain both of us here.'

She knew that, but she also knew whoever this Fabiola was, her taste in clothes was nothing like her own. It was flashy and Western. From a place of panic, she said to him, 'Let me help you.'

He began to rearrange his furniture, his shoes, his books before he turned back to look at her. 'Yes, that's all well and good, but how long are you here for? I have to register you with the local authorities. Speaking of which – didn't you have trouble with your pass? How did you get past the checkpoints?'

'I'm here to stay, Ba Charles. A man needs his helper just as much as a woman her protector. I want to have a family.'

Charles sat on his single spring bed. She did not give him a chance to object – again.

'I will sell these clothes for you while you go to work. I will cook and clean, so you can focus on why you came here.'

'But I'm too busy to look after you right now. Other than the school, I am responsible for the administration at the teacher's union. The amalgamation round tables are not looking up in our favour, and it looks like we might lose. They are going to turn Rhodesia into a federation with Nyasaland,

Margaret. If they do, we are done! These bastards won't rest until they turn us into another South Africa. Why would we want to start a family if we know that we are being ushered into an apartheid system with our eyes wide open? Give me a chance to sort that out first, then we can live together as man and wife.'

She cleared the trinkets on the small table and moved his typewriter slightly to the left. The rays from the sunset beamed across the room through a small window. Dust particles danced mid-air in the gap between them.

'Apatebeta Lesa tapafuka chushi. When God presents opportunities to us, my husband, He does so without fanfare. I will place my sewing machine here, and we will work side by side. You will not have to look after me.'

*

That night, bicycle bells chimed and jeering men returned from beerhalls. They made love how Charles preferred it. He unwrapped her nightgown and he kissed her with his mouth open. He made her moan when she was not supposed to.

Everything that he had never done before, he did.

That was the only time Margaret ever defied her husband.

CHAPTER 8

MAGGIE OLUWASEUN AYOMIDE
LUSAKA, ZAMBIA, 1992

ONE BLISTERING MORNING – after weeks of Mum disappearing mysteriously at night – she screams so loudly it feels like the stained ceiling boards in our apartment are going to crumble. The small, metal television with its long antennae plays celebratory songs from South Africa, from Zambia, from Congo.

It feels like it did last year when they freed the smiling man from South Africa, and he came to visit Zambia. He had asked to see Mum and Grandpa Charles. Nelson Mandela. I remember because when he came, Mum cleaned the house at least a dozen times. She moved me out of my room to hers, and we made a bed for Grandpa Charles with fluffy pillows and fresh pyjamas. We even put a jar of frangipani on the little dining table and I wrote a 'Welcome home, Grandpa' card from the both of us. She couldn't stop humming and she made sure she put enough petrol in her Cressida. She went away for two whole days, and on the third, she came back alone. Her car as empty as it was when she left.

Now, she's screaming the house down like she did that day. They said Mandela was arrested and kept on a scary island for 27 years. Now everyone on the television is talking about us having a new leader after 27 years of one-party democracy. It is all so confusing. What is so special about this number, 27? And how can one party be a democracy?

There is a short man on a stage behind a podium who speaks with his mouth upside down. He flutters his eyelids up to the sky, telling us in curly drawn-out English that he is willing to 'die for de-mo-cracy'. He repeats, like the people beyond the keyhole, that 'the hour has come!'

The overflowing crowd cheers. It swells with each moment.

He cries and wipes his eyes.

He is always crying on TV.

'Who is it, Mummy?'

'It's Frederick Chiluba, my baby! MMD has won the elections! It is time for change!'

'What change, mama?'

'Change in Zambia – freedom to speak our minds and to vote! It means we will see your grandfather soon. They will let him go!'

'Where is he?'

'I don't know, honey.' She clenches her fists.

'When he comes home, will we also see Uncle CJ and Uncle Kabaso – and Bupe and Aunt Jasmine?' I ask.

'I don't know, baby. Let's try to get this done first, eh? Kadan, kadan.'

I smile because she uses words my father used to. It means slowly, slowly. Gradual by gradual.

The short man who leads the crowd shouts, 'The hour?'

A dense sea dressed in baby blue responds:

'Has come!'

The call and response continues:

'Multiparty?'

'Menshi!'

'Inga wayitila pa mulilo?'

'Washima!'

I ask what he means in English. He is calling multi-party water. How can that be? Mum says it's a metaphor. And then, he says if you pour the water on fire, it will put it out. I ask her if it's OK because the advert we sing everyday says to do the right thing – to keep the flame burning.

'If we pour the water on the flame, will we still be the Promised Land?' I ask.

She laughs at me. 'We are the promised land already. We just have to make it work! This is our home! Chalo chesu!'

'Yes, our home.' I mouth. I still want it to be home. But deep in my heart, I know it is not my only home.

*

Grandpa Charles shuffles to the dining table for breakfast while his walking stick clicks against the concrete floor with each step he takes. He is so big that when he stands in the frame of the door, it looks like he needs a little nudge from the back to get through. His left eye is sealed shut. He wears a paisley cravat neatly folded at his neck, and it tucks into the collar of his white safari shirt. His trousers are creased with a sharp edge that runs down the middle to brown bedtime slippers.

It's been six months since we were led through the streets of Lusaka in cries of jubilation. Throngs of people waving leaves as we drive through. Lines of lilac coloured jacaranda trees in bloom flanked the black tarred roads, guiding the direction of our motorcade. Placards flashed outside the window: symbol of freedom – our hero. Police sirens and motorcycles led the way and followed us too. It's been six months since I felt the rush through my veins as the gates of State House opened for us. Soldiers saluted along a driveway towards a red-brick palace with peacocks gliding outside the main hall.

It's also been half a year that he hasn't said a word.

He sits at the head, and mother is at his right hand, me to his left. His bowl is enamel – stained dark blue around the rim. It turns yellow in the middle where aubergine coloured flower prints stare back at him. Ba Mailesi bends a flask to the middle of his bowl and a perfect circle of brown porridge begins to widen and widen until he makes a sign with his hand for her to stop. Millet. Mum says it's his favourite.

I kick the leg of the table, and Mum throws me a look. It is enough for me to heed warning. I sit up straight, and my own white pool of mealie meal porridge fills my porcelain bowl. We listen to each other in silence. Chewing is all I hear, and then swallowing. Large gulps pass down my grandfather's throat and his Adam's apple moves up and down his neck like an elevator.

He bends down and writes a note to Mum. She looks up from her newspaper shaking her head. 'We can call them again if you want, Tata, but CJ says that they can't come. He says it's not the right time.' She rolls her eyes and turns back to the pages in her newspaper. 'Whatever that means.' Grandpa looks outside the window. His face twists into a grimace before he wipes his mouth with his napkin. He clears his throat and takes a sip of his orange juice.

'It's time for me to head to Chinsali,' his voice rumbles. It is strong enough to lift the room and every item in it, to throw us out to yonder. Mum and I look at each other with a start, and then at him.

'I will go home. You ladies will move into the Woodlands house. Maggie, I am sure you will come to love it as much as your grandmother and I did. However, I expect to see you in the village at least once a year from now on. Do we have a deal?'

My heart beams bright rays of joy. 'We have a deal, Grandpa!'

CHAPTER 9

BUPE KOMBE
LONDON, UK, 1997

JEROME AND I SPEND every single afternoon together. It's the summer holidays, and the sun scorches the ground. In turn, the pungent smell of garbage balloons around us. We muck about his estate looking for ice cream for me and jerk chicken for him. Everyone sees us together and they ask us if we'll get married one day. Married? I'm way too young to be thinking about that. But Jerome is my best friend in the whole world.

'Roll with me today?' He winks at me.

'Where to?'

'I need to drop something off with one of my mates at his yard.'

'Who?'

'You don't know him. It'll only take a couple minutes and then we head right back, yeah?'

We cycle down the streets together. As we glide further, he leads me down some alleys I've never passed through before. We ride around discarded mattresses with people asleep on them.

'Jerome, it's well grime out here. Where are we going?'

'Don't worry. You're with me, babe. I got you.' He

presses the brakes on his bike, and I slow down next to him. 'Don't you trust me?'

'Yes, I do but …'

'No buts, babe. Together forever, remember? I got you, OK?'

We place our bikes against a wall with massive piss stains on it. 'Just do what I say, and whatever happens, stay put.'

He takes me by the hand, and we walk around the corner.

'Be back in a sec,' he says, planting me outside the window of a glittering pawn shop. Jerome walks only a few feet away, and a group of older boys come out to talk to him. With a quick swipe, he passes the tallest one something. I can't make it out from where I stand. The shorter one with his hair in cornrows down to his back places his arm around Jerome. He rubs Jerome's head in a big brother sort of way, but I've never seen him before. I look around. My denim shorts feel too short. There is a sudden chill in the wind. I make a gesture to cover myself with a coat, but I don't have one on. My reflection looks back at me, and so does the Indian man behind the counter.

Jerome is heading back in my direction. He bounces off his right foot with an exaggerated swagger that he doesn't normally have when he's alone with me. As he approaches, screeching tyres smoke down the street. His group scatters in all directions. A loud bang goes off into the air. I crouch with my hands to my ears and he runs towards me. He hurls himself across me and holds me to the ground while another car sprays bullets above our heads. His friends are gone.

My face is pressed hard to the ground. I can't breathe, but the concrete is my refuge. Even if I could, I'm too afraid to look. His body pushes on mine until there is complete silence. 'Run!' he says. We sprint to our bikes, and cycle. All the way back to his flat, I am sick with fear. I can't bring myself to look behind me. When we get to his place, I yell at him. 'What the hell was that, Jerome? Are you trying to get us killed?'

'How was I supposed to know that some geezer would roll

up and do a ting? I just needed to give my mate something, that's all! Must have been them African boys from Peckham, innit? They're on one lately.'

'I hate you!' I tremble from anger and fear.

He hugs me from behind and whispers in my ear. 'I'm sorry, B. I didn't know that would happen. I would never do anything to put you in danger. You feel me? Like, you're the best thing that ever happened to me.' He squeezes my waist tight. 'I love you. You're my everything.'

His hands slide up my belly. He rubs the skin softly to soothe me. His hands are hot on my taut skin They steal up higher to my breasts. He cups them. My body still quakes, but it begins to bend to his touch. He sucks and bites my neck, pausing only to peel off my tank top. He turns me around to face him, and we kiss. He rips off my shorts, and I lift his top over his shoulders. His jeans fall to a heap on the ground, and our bodies meet. Hearts racing, sweating, our bodies intertwine.

As he lays me on the bed, his door swings open.

*

Jerome's buxom mum drags him and me by our ears. From the corner of my eye, all I can see is her bearded chin. Jerome is as silent as a lamb being taken to the slaughter. He makes no attempt to speak up for us.

She marches us down Coldharbour Lane, up our street, and finally, all the way to my nan's doorstep – still by our ears. Onlookers jeer from their stalls – many clap and whistle. She swings open the door to the curry house, and the noise of the bell announces to all the patrons that we have come in.

'Ms. West!' she shouts, heaving and sweating.

'Why, hello, darling. What have you for me today?' My grandmother looks up, her silver strands of hair pinned back neatly into a bun.

'I want to let you know that I found these two in a

compromising position. In Jerome's bedroom! Having sex!' she hisses.

She crosses her heart and looks upwards, saying a quick prayer for us. 'But don't worry. I've beaten both of them for ya!'

'Thank you – I'm so sorry for the inconvenience. I'll talk to my girl, and you can talk to your boy. I'm sure we can settle this matter without causing too much scandal.' She sweeps her eyes over the staring guests.

'Hmm, OK, but if I catch 'em again, I won't go so easy next time! Mek sure to tell CJ and Jasmine so that I know we are on the same page. We are good folk. Wi cyaa ave dem yah pickney running around like dem nuh ave home! And, I should let you know that the only reason I rushed home early is because my cousin Carson Little. You know him, right? Well, his boy Gerald, yeah? His best mate says he saw them running away from a shooting earlier. No one is safe at all! Please, take your girl, me nuh wa trouble!'

I look to Jerome to see something, anything, from him, but he doesn't lift his eyes, not for a moment. I watch him leave with his mother, hoping that I will get to see him soon.

Later at night, I hear them deliberate the matter. Mum begs Dad behind the shut door to their kingdom upstairs. Hushed voices and pleading cries leave just enough to make out the conversation. I sit on the stair where I used to wait for them as a child. My fingers brush through the beige carpet in small circles.

'Let her go, CJ! She deserves to know her family.'

'I can't, Jas. You know how Stella feels about me. And what about Bupe? You want to send her to a place she's never been?'

'CJ, I have never grown up in Jamaica. I would have loved to, but I did not have that choice. Let her go. Let her see another side of life. Let her know where she comes from!'

'Exactly, choice. Are we giving her a say here?'

'We've got to make the decision for her before she makes

some big mistakes. Don't forget, we're losing young lives every day. I see it at the centres. The gangs have been growing, and their influence is getting stronger. If she continues to hang out with that Jerome boy – CJ, I'll never forgive you if something happens to her.'

I burst into their room to put an end to the discussion. 'Please, I'm sorry! You can't do this! You can't send me away because of one mistake. I have rights you know!' They look at me, both with eyes of steel. I look at Dad and he looks away.

'I'll be good – I promise!'

'You mean everything to us, Bupe, but sometimes the hardest decisions are the best ones we make. How could you be so foolish, endangering your life like that? What would we do if something happened to you? Was it Jerome's idea?'

'No! It was mine. It was all my fault.'

'Go to sleep,' my mother says, her patience wearing thin. 'We'll talk in the morning.'

*

My nan and I sleep in her bed, and she strokes my hair all night. Her room has always smelled of lavender and starched cotton sheets. My ear is crimson, still stinging from the walk of shame from Jerome's house. Flashbacks of his mum's bearded chin taunt me. Hot concrete against my face is what I feel again. Gunshots ring loud in my ears, and my heartbeat is the only sound that I hear. It is loud and fast. The thought of being so far away from my nan makes me move closer to her. The whole night I sleep in the shape of a C. I enjoy the rhythm of her breathing and the pudginess of her arms.

The next morning, it is settled. Phone calls and emails are exchanged, application forms filled in – I am being deported to Africa by my own family. I've known Brixton all my life, never been to the Midlands, and now, here I am about to be sent to the back of nowhere. I have to take slow breaths to stop myself from bolting out the door. The curry house is quiet. Nan hasn't played any music today. I sit at my bedroom window looking out into our street. I look for Jerome, hoping he'll come and speak up for me. Make this whole mess go away.

Grandpa Charles says our trust will cover my tuition. A trust though. How posh! It's never ever occurred to me that I could fall in the 'trust fund baby' bracket. He says I can spend holidays with him at the farm or with my cousin, Maggie, and – dare I say it – Aunty Stella, the Ice Queen. My father and her don't speak to each other and now he's sending me to her lair? Dad is the only one who is unhappy about the trust, nor has he ever mentioned it to me. But then again, Dad is unhappy about all the cool things to do with his family.

In between sniffles and kisses, I say goodbye to my nan. I hold on to her tightly. When it's time to go, she unwraps my arms from her shoulders and plants a kiss on my forehead. I ask her what she thinks of them sending me away and she chirps quietly. 'When cockroach go party, him no ask fowl. Let Jerome be. Go on this journey to find your people and your greatness. If your paths are meant to cross again, they will.'

CHAPTER 10

MAGGIE OLUWASEUN AYOMIDE
LUSAKA, ZAMBIA, 1997

OUR WOODLANDS HOME is a tapestry of untold tales. We have lived here since I was ten. It has beautiful gnarled trees that hold hands and talk to each other. I know this because I hear them whisper when I listen hard enough. The older ones with the chequered bark and deep groves have both wonderful and sad stories for the younger ones with firm green skins. The dense sound of crickets mixes with the twittering of birds and the shuffling of leaves. It is so comforting in the daytime. The manicured kapinga carpet is dappled from the light that makes its way through the shade of the large trees. The jut-jut-jut of automated sprinklers makes droplets of water dance in a grand display of synchronised, circular motions. Garden boys spray their hosepipes as they lie on their backs with caps on their faces when they think we can't see them.

'Bupe is a wild mess.' My mother scowls over a letter from Uncle CJ while the maid brings in a steaming cup of tea. 'She's a melting pot waiting to explode! I don't know why on earth CJ would choose to raise a child in Brixton when he should be here running our estate and managing your grandfather's affairs.' The maid scurries back along the red brick veranda and bypasses the indoor courtyard.

My mother has filled it with all manner of exotic succulents and palm fronds, and the streaming light from its glass roof makes an exquisite display in her lobby. Sometimes I imagine my grandparents having tea and crumpets in there, listening to a wiry man in coat tails play the piano. Other times, I see her floating down the stairs in something shimmery, like she's always appeared since I was little.

The laughter of children on the other side of our fence distracts me. I hear them making cannonballs as they blast into their swimming pool. I look at our own. It is covered neatly with stretched canvas. It has been empty for decades.

Mum says it's too expensive to maintain. 'Besides, swimming should be for discipline and fitness, not for leisure. It would be an injustice to the world if you could just lie in the water all day like a hippo.' I hope that when Bupe comes, we can share stories and have fun like the kids next door too.

'I'm sure it will make Grandpa happy to have her here.'

'Yes, I suppose it will.'

My stomach churns with anticipation. I run to my room, and I practice our first greeting. My English accent is many years gone, hardened, buried far below my subconscious with firm Zambian vowels.

Every now and then, my mother chides me. 'Remember, don't place the wrong "emphasis" on the right "syllable", Maggie.' I think of Bupe, and I try to reach deep inside to find it. What if she won't understand me? Or what if she thinks I'm not cool enough? I look in the mirror to practice.

'Oyi. Hello. Pleasure to meet you cousin?' I repeat this, and two of the ladies who clean the house fall through the crack of my door chuckling at me. I fling a giant teddy bear at them, but they come back heaving. I fold my arms and face the window, my lower lip hanging low. 'Maggie, just be yourself, mama. She will love you the way you are, wamvela?' They poke my ribs and we erupt in cackles. I hope what they are saying is true. I couldn't be English if I tried. Ba Mailesi joins us, and she ties a chitenge around her waist. She advances towards me, moving her hips from side to side. She dips her hands as though to lift the earth and she raises them towards the sky. Her eyes twinkle as she calls me to dance with her. She claps through a happy song for me, singing:

My heart is full of joy this day. My child has finally found her sister. All these years she has been alone. Father let her find joy in the family you have given her. Give her laughter all the rest of her days …

*

Each night I count the sleeps left until she arrives. I dream of Heathrow.

We are running, the lights blinding us. I see adult feet. Moving, sprinting. We are running away from being a family. I leave something behind. A book, a pen, a photograph. I can't go back to get it. The gates are shut tight. I cry, begging them to let me back in, but they cannot hear me. My voice is locked deep down in my belly. I try to shout for Dad. Nothing comes out of my mouth. With all my strength I draw on every inch of breath in my being. I shout, 'Bupe!' My voice finally is set free.

I wake up. My pillow is soaking wet.

*

We wait for her at the Lusaka International Airport arrivals. I look at my mother's face, and I can tell that she would rather clamber up the stairs to heaven right now, than have to deal with another pubescent teenager in her house. Beads of sweat appear along her nose. She wipes her bald head with a handkerchief and pats her skirt down. She repeatedly twists her malachite ring. Her copper bangles clang at each other.

We wait and wait. She tugs at my pink balloon dress to straighten it, and she does a double take because I have a small stain on my ballerina pumps. Mum says people have forgotten how to dress for the airport. She believes in putting your best foot forward especially when you are flying because you never know who you will meet. 'Whenever you travel, you represent both family and country.'

I really wish I could be clad in jeans, but Ba Mailesi and Mum and all the house help said I needed to make a good first impression. I stand here now, my dress gripping my torso. It makes me breathless. Its coarse texture makes me itch. My skirt puffs out at the sides. A man behind me keeps his sunglasses on, and I'm certain it's from the glare coming off my skirt.

A family who is holding a round cake with too much blue piping and zigzag patterns on it, bring the airless room down with throaty ululations for a returning medical student from Russia. We know this because we've spent enough time here and they have eagerly told everyone who is waiting. "First doctor in this family. First one to travel abroad!" his mother says, announcing through chequered teeth. Mum starts to murmur to herself because the Russian doctor looks like the last passenger.

Bupe eventually strolls out.

She's got her hair pulled back in a messy ponytail, and she's dressed in all black from head to toe except for a Che Guevara type camouflage green jacket. Her black leggings show off her long legs and are wrapped in calf high Dr. Martens. She's laughing into the air with all the staff from the luggage area who are pushing her baggage for her. To my mother's horror, she's offering fist pumps and high fives to all of them, talking about 'reppin' her ends in the Sarrf.'

When Mum thinks things are as bad as they could be, Bupe lunges at her for a long kiss and a cuddle. Mum appears mortified. I am in stitches holding it all inside. It's so juicy to watch from the corner of my eye. It's hilarious, but the last thing I want to do is have Mum mad at me when Bupe has just arrived. So, I stare straight on at the wall which has been brushed in oil paint the colour of milk gone bad. I focus on the triangular bit that's still water paint, egg yolk yellow, because someone must have forgotten to finish the job. I take in my brand new cousin's bear hugs, and I won't say it aloud, but if I had to try on that English accent, I would say, 'it feels frickin' awesome to have her here!"

Our eyes catch, and we smile. I see a glaze in my cousin's eyes, and I blink a few times myself. Mother would be flabbergasted if I dissolved into tears in public. Bupe is squeezing my hand. She smells like cocoa butter and peppermint.

'Your dress is pretty.' She looks so London cool. I feel like a pink pumpkin in the sun.

'Thank you. I like your boots.'

'I can't believe I'm in Africa! Aunt Stella, I've been asking Dad to let me come since I was little.'

'You are welcome, Bupe. Let's get going so we can settle you in at home.'

*

Bupe finds school to be easy, mostly because anyone will do anything for her. She has a charm that is impossible to turn down. Her laugh is infectious and her wit uncanny. Our teachers reel at first, probably because they are not used to being bombarded by questions from students. Religious studies is the worst because Bupe is armed with all manner of philosophy and accurate detail.

Having her around gives me a sense of family outside of me and Mum for the first time since I was young. But I have to be extra careful because I have a puff adder for a cousin it seems. Like the time she finished doing her laundry in the courtyard and went to hang her school shirts on the line, she overheard some girls speaking behind billowing linen, oblivious to their eavesdropper.

'Maggie feels like the popular girl now that she has a cousin from London in school.'

'Yes, I've noticed how she doesn't say hi to me lately. In

fact, she's always been a bit weird and distant, but now I figure she's just a pompous bi—'

Bupe didn't let them finish. She splashed a bucket of dirty soapy water on them, and in their words, she told them 'to sod off'. A fight broke out, and she took them down, rolling in soapy mud, fists out like a boy. Fortunately, the news didn't get as far as the matron's office. We held court in the common room. If it had gone any further, they all would have been sent back home, and I don't know how Mum, or her parents would feel about her being expelled as soon as she arrived. More so, we would both be in trouble, even if I wasn't there.

I write in my journal before bedtime:

Dear God,
Thank you for giving me a wonderful cousin who cares so much about me. Help me to manage her because I don't want her getting in the way of my promise.
Still have to find Dad. Maybe uncle CJ will be able to help.

CHAPTER 11

BUPE KOMBE
LUSAKA, ZAMBIA, 1997

NINE HOURS. IT TAKES that much time to find yourself on the other side of the world. It takes less than a full day to find a brand-new life. If there were any cameras in my head or on the plane, I think I would have been escorted right back to London. However, by the time I got off the plane, my eyes were no longer red from crying over Jerome. I bit my nails to the quick as I anticipated meeting Maggie, and of course Aunty Stella too. Our first meeting at the Lusaka airport was me hugging and kissing these beautiful, dark, slender statues. I stopped when I realised how uncomfortable it made them feel. All the way home, I babbled about Mum and Dad and Nan, and Uncle Kabaso, and coming to Africa for the first time. I got little more than, "Oh, how nice" and, "Hmm, I see," as we drove round the roundabouts – there're plenty of those, and the perforated roads are terribly skinny.

I can't help but watch her. She's so mechanical and organised, that cousin of mine. For such a young person, she has a stoic air of endurance and a face that's slender and pretty but also grim, like the little glimpse I got of Aunty Stella when I arrived. Their home's perfect and colour coded – their books are stacked by height, tallest to shortest and back to tallest, creating perfect concaves along their walls. Nothing's placed without precise symmetry or intention, and no one wakes up a second after 6.00 a.m. She has house help that respond to her call, and she seems more comfortable being with them than she does her mother.

Maggie and Aunty Stella have a stealthy way of staying away from each other. I've never felt anything as awkward as when they are in a room at the same time. I don't think they ever touch or cuddle. They have one photograph of Grandma Margaret, and it's a portrait of her in the back of a beautiful black car; an Impala. Another one of Grandpa Charles stands next to hers, but it looks more official and serious, like a blown up passport photograph stuffed into a too small rectangular frame. Combing their walls for photographs makes me immeasurably sad. There's no evidence that they have any other family in this world, now or before.

Maggie is a year younger than me, but we are in the same grade. She shows me everything I need to do. At first, I sulk and whinge because I still can't believe how far my parents have sent me. Ba Mailesi greets me every morning from the floor of the kitchen veranda. Her face is menacing, old and wrinkled like a leather hide. She sits barefoot on a wooden stool, peeling cassava with a machete that glints against the morning sun – smiling at me. She always makes sure that I get more than enough food, and she pulls my cheeks like I'm a toddler. "Where is your chitenge?" she asks, but I simply shrug.

On my first morning here, she gave me a chitenge from Aunt Stella. Said I shouldn't go downstairs in my nightie or short shorts without it. Like, how ancient is that sort of thinking? I have never worn it. It sits, folded crisply – it's got guinea fowl randomly placed against a beautiful turquoise and green backdrop. I think I'd rather frame it for the world to see.

At school, the morning starts with lights being turned on at an ungodly hour by a tiny matron with a rude shock of grey hair. My roommate stands there staring at me when I ask her something. The ground shakes as a swarm of girls in flipflops and muffin shaped shower caps race to get into the showers first. The air is sliced with the sound of water smashing into buckets on concrete floor. They fill them with hot water for their mates who are still asleep. Maggie used to save one for me in the first few days, until she said I needed to become more 'independent'. 'If you want hot water, Bupe, you're going to have to wake up early like the rest of us. It's simple: wake up early, hot water – wake up late, cold shower – and worse, you'll be the last one in there after everyone's done their business. Your call.' I shudder at the thought of her last words.

The showers don't spray water because the shower heads got lost yonks ago, and the water on the floor rises to your ankles. Each time the cold water runs, I lather up completely so that I am left with no choice. I stand there looking at it until I feel I must look like a right nitwit, scared of this tiny challenge. I jump under it, and my body quakes. I yelp from the shock to my skin. 'Bloody Hell!' But after a few minutes, it's all over. And guess what? I'm clean and fresh, energised for the day.

In the dorm, just when I'm getting lotion on my body, the gong rings for breakfast, and I'm obviously late. I rush as quickly as I can. Hair tied back like my nan, smart shirt, I slip my tie over my head because Maggie did a Windsor knot for me in advance. She waits for me, impatiently, though, because she doesn't like to be late.

The dining hall is big and warm. The smell of milky tea and buttered toast fills the room. Everyone stops to stare at me, the clink clink of cutlery to plates ends suddenly and resumes after 30 seconds. Do I look that different? Or is it something they do for everyone who is new? While in the straight file to the kitchen, I hold a brown plastic tray and tin cup in both hands, and I ask Bupe why they stare.

She confirms that I look different, and yes, everyone who is new gets 'analysed'. 'Where does she come from? Look at her hair. And her shoes,' they will say, 'but don't worry,' she says, 'I'm sure you'll have plenty of friends. Girls like you never have a problem being popular.' Her words zap me, but I try not to show it because I'm desperate for her love. I always have been though she has no inkling.

On Tuesdays, the mailbox is emptied, and I'm so excited because my perfumed letters are on their way to Jerome. By then, I've probably put three in for him each week, describing in detail every aspect of this strange place. Every Friday, I watch the letter sack arrive fat, full of secret messages for everyone. Gradually it shrinks as stamped envelopes are handed to shrieking girls. Swooning teenagers feign malady or faint while their friends fan them, and they read all the juicy contents of the page to each other. Some run into a toilet booth to read in private, others cry – but nothing comes from Jerome.

My mother writes in blocks of all capitals. She only ever writes that way. Dad, on the other hand – his handwriting is flowery and slanted. I hesitate to read the letter because I know already what she is going to say. She writes:

IT IS TERRIBLY SAD, BUT I'M AFRAID JEROME HAS FOUND BROTHERHOOD AMONGST A CRIMINAL GANG AT THE ESTATES. BUPE, FOR YOUR OWN WELL-BEING, LOOK FORWARDS. ENJOY THE PRIVILEGE OF YOUR NEW START, AND FORGET THE BOY. THE WORLD HAS BIGGER PLANS FOR YOU. OUR EXPECTATIONS OF YOU, MY SWEET DAUGHTER, ARE AS HIGH AS ALL THE GREAT PEOPLE IN HISTORY WE HAVE TAUGHT YOU ABOUT.

All through prep, I scribble over her words, in hope that having them erased from this earth will make the burning image of him surrounded by dangerous people go away. What if he gets hurt? Has anyone thought about that? It's not his fault that no one was there for him – well except me. And he was always there for me too. They just don't understand him. He will come right. If I don't fight his corner, who will?

The bell sounds. I crumple up the messy letter, and I toss it into the bin.

*

People actually kumbaya around here. We have volunteers from all over the world in soft sandals and airy bohemian trousers. Many of them seldom take a shower. They make us practice a virtue every week. This week is 'tolerance'. If you act out of virtue, you get a demerit. I write it in my letter to Jerome, laughing at that. Like which one of his Yardie mates would give a shit about a flippin' demerit, and who in their right mind would understand 'tolerance' if they were disrespected? Like surely, there's got to be some exceptions to the rule.

The girls here are fabulous though. They love my accent and my clothes. I'm tempted to tell them that Mel B is my aunty. The teachers, on the other hand, are not so super – I have never known the real meaning of strict until here. The classes I am exceptional in are literature and modern history – oh, and art goes without saying.

Thanks to my parents, by age 10, I was reciting stanzas from Claude McKay and Linton Kwesi Johnson. By 11, I was questioning them, analysing their metaphors, translating their cinematic imagery, and breaking them down to create my own poetry. Aunty Stella says someone forgot to code modesty into our DNA. I think she means hers, and maybe mine, 'cause Maggie and my dad are shy as hell.

At the weekends, after prep, we sweep, mop, and wax the

floors of the dining hall. After the white cobra has hardened on the grey concrete, we break up our group into sections to lash at the floor with brushes and dry cloths. We shine and shine and shine, until the floor is gleaming, mirroring our faces. Maggie and the other girls prefer to do it on all fours. I insisted, at first, that it was better with my foot, until my thigh began to burn through, and I howled with the wrenching pain that tore right through my muscles.

Later, we are allowed to sign out our CD player from the dorm matron. Maggie and I lie down, exhausted, but in a good way, the kind you get from doing hard work and doing it well. We lie on her top bunk, an earphone bud in each ear, sharing music and mapping out our futures. Tuck spread from our tins between us – Crunchie chocolates, Eet-SumMor biscuits, brands from here that I'm learning to love. I suck and chew on a long pink Fizzer.

'I wish I had stayed in London with my mum and dad still together.'

I am startled by her words. She never speaks about family.

'Really? I wasn't sure at first, but now I wish I had been sent here earlier without my mum and dad. This place calms me, you know.

'Like, I've never known life could be so still. There're no police asking dumb questions as we walk home. There're no placards of protest to make. Here, we are first-class citizens because we're in our country? You feel me?'

She nods her head slowly. 'I think I know what you mean. When I was younger, that was one of the first things that struck me when we moved here. All of a sudden, I wasn't a minority anymore – well if you're talking skin colour.'

'Do you feel like a minority because of anything else?'

'Well, no, just different.'

'How?'

'Everyone else has a family. They come from here. I do come from here, but I come from Nigeria too.'

'Can you go there, to see your dad?'

'I don't know where he is, Bupe.'

'He's out there somewhere. He'll turn up sooner or later, and if he doesn't, I'll help you find him. We are family, and that's what family does, right?' She turns the other way.

Usher Raymond's solitary poster is on her wall. It looks like a red carpet moment with a fade out of a backdrop and bright lights behind him. Maggie is so tame because my wall has Mase, Puffy, Prince William, Richard Blackwood, and if any of them proposed to me today I would scream a yes. If all of them proposed, the answer would still be affirmative, but of course, it would become a last man standing kinda ting.

Maggie asks me what Uncle Kabaso is like. She speaks to him once a year on his birthday.

'Well, for starters, he's not straight.'

'He's not what?'

'He's gay,' I say, 'he likes men.'

Maggie says she's never met 'a gay'. I tell her there's plenty in London. Whenever Mum and Dad are consumed with another world ending emergency, it's Uncle Kabaso who takes me to the city. To Trocadero, to Soho, to the carnival in the summer. He lets me be me, and he is the best person in the world to shop with. He taught me how to do the butterfly when I was 11, the weird dance that looked and felt like it was made up until everyone was doing it. 'Come on then. Legs in and out, round, and snap!' he would say in his baggy pants and a striped Malcolm X t-shirt.

He keeps all my secrets, and he tells me his. I lower my voice to reveal it. After all, Maggie is family. She's my sister.

'His biggest secret is that he is too scared to come home.' I turn to look at her.

'But why?' She stops chewing her eclair and sits up to look back at me.

'I don't know. He doesn't feel at home here, I guess. He says London is home.'

'But we are from Chinsali!'

'Yeah, but would they understand a man who loves to

sing and dance on stage and dates men too? And when I say dance, Maggie, Uncle Kabaso is so gifted. His work makes you wanna cry, or sing, or whatever. It makes you wanna do something bigger than what's around you!'

'Well, for your eyes to change colour like that, he must really move you,' Maggie says. 'Maybe we should talk to Grandpa and ask him to bring him home.'

'No use. Uncle Kabaso is happy there. Not a word to the old man, please. I don't know if he knows. I'm too scared to meet Grandpa. It's like Dad can't stand up straight when his name is mentioned.'

Maggie laughs. 'He's tough, it's true, but he's loving. I know he can't wait to spend time with you. You'll love him.'

*

Eventually, Maggie and I discover that we work best together. We climb to the top of class. We work hard and dream hard. She helps me in chemistry and maths, showing me how to calculate moles and masses. I break down Petruchio's character from 'Taming of the Shrew' and expound the symbolic use of the fiend in Mary Shelley's 'Frankenstein'. Our names on the weekly scoreboard climb steadily and hold their position – we hold hands every Friday afternoon as we wait for our results to come up. We become house captains, and we return home laden with sparkling trophies.

CHAPTER 12

MAGGIE OLUWASEUN AYOMIDE
CHISAMBA, ZAMBIA, 1997

IN PREP, BUPE SCRIBBLES black ink all over her mother's letters. She crushes them into tiny balls and tosses them carelessly into a bin on our way out of class. The first time she did that, it bothered me, but I thought perhaps it was just the one time. Last week, she got another one. A beaming red envelope with three stamps in a row that had a crowned Queen Elizabeth looking at the back of her own head. It had fancy cursive writing on the front, which I've known since I was little is Uncle CJ's.

She opened it. She read it, laughing here and there until she became silent. She read it again. At first, she bit her nails until she grabbed a felt tip from my desk and squiggled away at what I imagined to be beautiful, loving messages from her mum and dad. When the bell rang, my feelings were so intensified that I pushed her against the door on my way out of class. She ran after me. I was standing under the large tree outside our bland, shapeless dining hall. Its branches moved to and fro as the wind grew stronger. Gaggles of girls streamed past us, and the dark sky sat close.

'What is it, Maggie?'

'Why would you do that?'

'Do what?'

'Why would you do that to letters from your own mother? You have a mum and a dad who write you every single week!'

'So?' Her scarf flapped hard against her blazer. I had to raise my voice.

'I would do anything to hear from them. What did they do today? Where did they go? Who did they see? I have one parent who vanished into thin air when I was eight, and another one who has her own life without me in it!'

'Just because mine are married doesn't mean they see me, Maggie.'

'Bupe, they do. If they can write you every week, then they do see you.'

She lowered her eyes. 'They want me to forget Jerome, and I can't imagine life without him. Maggie, he's my best friend.'

'Well, if he's your best friend, why hasn't he written you? Why is he there, and why are you here? Didn't you get into trouble because of him? Has he even said sorry?'

We both had tearless eyes because of the wind, but we could feel each other crying. I felt bad for making her sad, but I desperately need to ask her one question. 'Do you think he can help me find him?'

'Jerome? Find who?'

'No. Uncle CJ. Do you think your dad can help me find my dad?'

She looked at me, hands in pockets. 'If you want my dad to help you find him, you've got to make your mother speak to him. To do that, you've got to be willing to do something ballsy to get her attention.'

'No, not ballsy.' I covered my mouth with my hands.

She stepped forwards to remove them for me, and she gripped my wrists tightly.

'Why not?'

'I made a promise a long time ago. Once I graduate, I'll turn 18 and then I'll be able to look for him.'

'You don't get extra points for being a goody-two-shoes your whole life. Speak up for yourself, Maggie. Let's run away! Let's go, fam. Come with me now and help me get back to London. If you go missing, she'll come looking for you, and you can negotiate your terms and conditions. Me? I'll call the socials and tell them my family wants to send me back against my will.'

I looked into her eyes and felt my heart beat wildly. My mouth was dry. Suddenly, it was just her and I on this lone planet. If her plan worked, I would either die from the shame of doing something so grossly irresponsible – or I would live a little bit more? Feel alive? And maybe, just maybe, I would actually find him.

'OK, Bupe, but what about money? And how do we get out of here? We need a car, passports.'

'We ain't got none, cuz!' Bupe laughed and laughed. A flash of rage engulfed me before the honey glow of her eyes warmed my soul.

'I thought you were serious!'

We looked at the high walls layered with garlands of barbed wire and the spotlights planted throughout the gardens that shifted their lights from shrub to shrub.

'Look, Maggie, we'll stick to your plan, but I will ask Dad to talk to Aunt Stella, and let's see if they can find him, yeah? And I promise, cross my heart, to not throw their letters away but you have to promise to help me get back to Jerome too.'

'No, I don't. That's so different!'

CHAPTER 13

BUPE KOMBE
CHINSALI, ZAMBIA, 2001

ON GRADUATION DAY, Grandpa comes to see Maggie and me do our victory dance down the aisle of the recreation hall in our black gowns and caps. Some idiot decided it should be the instrumental to Tupac's 'Changes'. Last year the seniors used R. Kelly's 'I Believe I Can Fly'. What a piss take. We might as well whine down to Shaggy's 'Mr. Boombastic', innit? In a single file, we step left and right, and we twirl. I feel so silly but seeing how elated everyone is makes me join the giggles.

Grandpa's glowing from the front row – smile plastered on permanently and all. When I take the podium to give the speech for our year, he stands and claps enthusiastically, which makes everyone do the same, and here in Chisamba, the place I was so afraid of coming to, is where I have my first standing ovation. He wipes his eyes with a white handkerchief, and this makes both Maggie and me well up. Aunty Stella is attending a women's empowerment conference in Beijing, so she can't be with us.

Afterwards, there's a lot of fuss around him. They can't believe he's come, that they've seen him in the flesh.

Dad says he was a tough man. But with Maggie and me, he's the best grandfather two girls could ask for. A soft, huggable grandpa who listens. He's not so understanding when it comes to failure, so I'm glad that we've both done well in school. Grandfather says we are named after the love of his life. He calls us his wives.

We go to Chinsali with him for the third time in my life. It's a long drive. It takes 12 hours from Lusaka on a good day with perfect weather and a good car.

A long, modern bungalow made of glass sits atop a hill in the middle of an isolated village. The misty rolling hills are green at Christmas time. Verdant foliage in the form of umbrella shaped trees ripple through the mountains, cut by meandering streams, and one long, tarred road.

It's full of memories, a shrine almost – to him and grandmother, to the family life they built. His library is large with a typewriter on a steel desk – Shonga Steel – reminiscent of 1980s Zambia. Next to it is a little desk with a Singer sewing machine. The walls are lined with Encyclopedia Britannica collections, each full of facts going as far back as 1910. There are law records from the 1960s, books, and report cards from my father's days in primary school.

His leather binoculars stand on his desk. He comes strapping through the doors of his bedroom, bellowing, summoning us to view the hills from his veranda. When I look through them, I get to see Chinsali through his eyes. Paradise right here on earth. At times, a lone cyclist passes by, and because the village is so small, everyone knows exactly who it is. The sound of axes chopping wood stops. The jarring motor from the sawmill stops. All chores stop. Everyone shades their eyes from the sun to discuss who it is and what business they may have in the BOMA – British Overseas Management Administration. They all wave at the cyclist even though he can't see them.

The night is thick as a cloak – it wraps my body until I'm invisible. I can't see the outline of my own hand in front of me once the lights go off, even though the stars hang low and burn brightly.

In the morning, we rise to the sound of a beat, of orchestrated music. Alternating pounding of knee high, hip wide, mortar and pestles. The sound of loose grain being sieved in large open baskets and tossed into the air to let the wind take the chafe away. Roosters and hens are let out of their home, which sits high on wooden stilts to protect them from twisting pythons. They climb down their stairs elegantly and cluck away while the babies on the backs of the ladies sorting beans for storage, make gurgling sounds. Smoke from fires outside is prelude to the munkoyo, a maize drink from a tasty root that is made for visitors. Later, we will drink it in pastel tin cups while we chew on the grainy bits inside. I don't know how I can ever explain this magic to Jerome or any of my mates back home.

When it rains, colourful buckets, striped cake tins, bowls, anything that can collect the pouring water from rippling timber roofs are lined up. Children dance barefoot in the rustcoloured water. Thunderstorms are deafening, but everyone smiles because it means there'll be food to eat and water to do their chores.

When it's sunny, Maggie and I use the outside bathroom to take a bath. A thatched, square wall with sky above and a bucket of soft rainwater's all we need. The birds in the trees fly over us as we take turns to make sure no one's coming. We enjoy the sun on our backs as we get dressed. The inside of each eyelid burns red when I close my eyes towards the sun. I let it kiss me and fill me with a power that I have never felt anywhere else before.

In the afternoon, we line up our old batteries on the windowsill so they can soak up the sun and – boom! – we have enough new energy to use our CD player. Grandpa takes us to a hidden waterfall 30 minutes from home. It has cascading curtains of water and mist. There is no one else here. It feels like a marvellous secret we get to share among the three of us.

'These waterfalls have tremendous power. To give beauty. To give light. To heal the sick. Once they are discovered for commercial use, it is our responsibility to ensure that the right choices are made. Do you understand me?'

'Yes, Grandpa.' We follow the footpath along the falls and enjoy the twitter of the birds in the woods. 'Geez, can you imagine how David Livingstone must have felt when he first saw the Victoria Falls? I bet you he did somersaults and cartwheels, screaming, "Mama I made it!"'

Maggie laughs, but a serious look takes a hold of her face. 'I can't believe we have resources like this, so hidden and unused.'

'Dr Livingstone found the Mosi-oa-Tunya, and he named it after his queen. Don't let them tell you that he discovered it. It has always been there and a part of the lives of the people there, the Tonga, the Batoké – they described it as the Smoke that Thunders way before he did those cartwheels.'

On Sundays, Grandfather, Bupe, and I dress smartly. He takes us to church in his Land Rover. He says he doesn't believe in it, but he says my grandmother would have liked for us to go to Lubwa Mission. It has a red brick building with a tall steeple, beneath which is boldly engraved, '1934, LUBWA MISSION,' the year the Church of Scotland built it. Glassless windows let the air flow freely in and out of the church. It has simple wooden benches, and some bricks for the congregation to sit on. Bright pink bougainvillea flowers grow into the church through the windows. Wasps with yellow and black stingers buzz in and out, arduously building homes of red sand in the corners of the church. Transparent geckos crawl across the walls, and every now and then, the service is disturbed when one falls onto a member of the congregation. It delights the children, and everyone sets off in laughter.

He sits at his favourite spot, the last row on the left.

'Your grandmother – I used to watch her from here. So beautiful and strong she was. Just like the two of you.' His voice is unusually deep, and it has a nasal quality to it.

Maggie and I cut bunches of bougainvillea for the reverend's service. I call him Rev Run, and Maggie does that weird thing she does by looking away because she doesn't want to get into trouble, but I know she's having a laugh. She's probably trying to keep herself from imagining him spinning a record and spitting on a mic. Having said that, his performance when we attend is particularly melodramatic. Bemba hymns are led by a two step conductor who lurches into the air with each note he instructs. He bends down low, swinging his bottom like a hammock when the bass is brought in, and on soprano he spins in delight. His choir is synchronised, and even Maggie can't hold it in on this one. We look sideways to each other and let the laughter bubble up and flow out. Grandpa gives us a pinch each, and it makes us fart from our mouths instead.

During the service, I look around. Little children are in tattered hand-me-down party dresses or their dad's torn t-shirts with nothing inside. They look at us as though we are from a planet far away. Hands on chin, they glower at us, ignoring the words of Rev Run. We tell them to come closer, and they do, but still they regard us as foreign creatures, something unusual in their world. So bizarre that they speak English and go to school. They wear clean clothes and have neat ponytails and friendship bracelets. They have a grandfather rattling in a whole big glass house to himself, plenty of books and pictures. They stare at these creatures in wonderment.

'He is a father to the fatherless! A defender of widows! Repeat after me!' He shouts in Bemba, 'I said, He is a father to the fatherless. Turn with me to Psalms 68:5.' Rev Run thunders out to the congregation. Maggie sits up. Her eyes burn on the man at the front. She flips the pages in her Bible until she finds the verse. She fixes her eyes on the passage for the rest of the service, and she places her marker on that page. Rev Run holds her in a powerful trance until it is finally time to go.

*

Grandfather shows us where our great grandparents are buried. The broken, leaning slabs of concrete scare me because they look like they'll sink into the ground. The 'Thriller' video's a real possibility from the look of the sunken slabs. Only this time, it would be Chinsali ghosts with no Michael Jackson to lead the choreography, just the overzealous conductor and Rev Run. Maggie and I pick the weeds around their graves and say a quiet prayer for these ancestors we never knew.

We sit at grandmother's grave, the only one still intact. He visits her every week. It is soft against the others because of its colour. White marble bordered with white stones. It has a well-tended rose bush at the foot. I stroke the smooth marble, and it is cold. Hard. He calls some boys to give us containers of water. As he picks the weeds from the damp soil, we speak to him.

'What was she like, Grandpa?' I ask.

'She was beautiful. She was intelligent. And she loved me so much.' He says this, but he winces.

'Was she from Lubwa too?' I push on.

'Yes, she was. We met here before we moved around the country and finally to Lusaka. Actually' – he laughs – 'I met her at the river. She was with her friends drawing some water, and I asked for some. Of course, she didn't give me any!

'She was a true traditionalist. She grew up with her parents and siblings. Her father was a teacher's assistant which, in those days, made them fairly comfortable in comparison to the rest of the village. Myself, I didn't have family. I lost my mother and father to a terrible fight they had when I was a little boy. My little brother died in a fire.'

'That's terrible, Grandpa. So, who did you live with?'

'I was raised by a Scottish missionary. A wonderful man who became like a father to me – though I still had to work to earn my stay. He taught me about the world. I learned to love Europe as much as I did Africa.'

'As a freedom fighter, I would think you wanted away with Europeans?'

'Well, I do believe in democracy and sovereignty first. There is no reason under the sun to justify the oppression of a human being by another. Unfortunately, it is a repeated theme in world history, even among the same race or tribe. So yes, to stand for my country's freedom was a clear and fierce conviction, that still remains. What happened thereafter is left to debate. Even after momentous milestones like abolition or independence, we suffer from intra-racial conflict. Some Caribbean people, for instance, feel that intra-racial issues are a direct result of being uprooted from Africa, totally cut off from their lineage. The coloureds in South Africa claim a similar malady, the Aboriginals in Australia and Canada have other kinds of issue, being minority groups on their own soil. The effects of oppression from former regimes will be felt for a long time to come. The issues did not disappear magically when we reclaimed our countries, it amazes me that we once thought we could make it all go away.' He stabs at the ground with his small garden fork.

'The important thing is that we now have our destiny in our own hands. It is up to you ladies to carry the mantle. What are you going to do for your country? For your generation and the ones who will come after you? We are responsible for finding our own solutions unique to our issues.'

Maggie and I hold hands. She bites her lip. She's been silent since the service ended. Finally, she speaks.

'When I was young, you were gone for a long time. Why won't anyone tell us what happened? I mean I know you were taken away by the government, but where were you?'

'I was taken away, Maggie. Sometimes, I was blindfolded for days, and carried around in a truck. Many times, I had no idea where I was.'

'Is that how you hurt your eye, Grandpa?' I ask.

His silence is heavy, and I regret the question.

'That chapter is closed now. I don't like to talk about it. But yes.'

Maggie presses on, and I want to grab her, to silence her.

'Grandpa, How did she die?' She traces the lettering along the tombstone.

'My wife had an accident. She fell into the pool at home. I was not there to save her. Instead, I was busy trying to save a country.' He turns his glance upwards. 'The sun is setting soon. We should head back.'

Maggie and I look at each other. I know she has questions running through her mind, because mine are plenty. I look around me, kids playing in the sand. The beautiful glassless church with its choir waving goodbye to one another. Grandpa's question rings sharply, 'What will you do for your country?'

CHAPTER 14

GRANDMOTHER MARGARET
COPPERBELT, NORTHERN RHODESIA, 1954

MARGARET KEPT HER FOOT on the baby's cradle, steady rocking it while she orchestrated her production team. The NR trio assembled red and black cloth badges for the AntiFederation Action Committee. One of them filled a steel iron with hot coals to press the final cuts down. It made the room uncomfortably warm. Charles stroked his new beard before he finished the last sentence on his latest article for the Freedom Newsletter. He rolled out the piece of paper before he reached for his scotch.

Murmurs arose from outside the house where youth from the Action Group were drinking Chibuku. A young man stepped inside to make an announcement to his leader. 'Mr. Kombe, you have guests, sir.'

Margaret and Charles's home had whirred activity the past few months. Men and women came in and out in droves, some crying, others asking for assistance with money, many delirious and wounded. None of the narrations were new to Margaret anymore. If it wasn't loitering, it was the native poll tax. Young men who failed to produce their passes came through their doors beaten to an inch of unconsciousness.

So, when Fabiola and Thomas walked in, Margaret sat straighter in surprise. She patted her soft afro and crossed her ankles. The last couple of years, she had heard about this mysterious lady from the other side of the border but had never seen her in the flesh. She filled the small room like a film star: her make-up was flawless, and she had an alluring beauty spot to the left of her upper lip. She stood in the centre of Margaret's small house with a superfluous fur coat draped around her shoulders. The NR Trio stood to remove it and prepare a chair for her. She sat and pulled a cigarette from its box. She looked around and frowned when she saw the baby. She retracted the stick into its sleeve.

Margaret offered the guests some tea, but they declined politely.

'Something stiffer would be lovely. Charles, could I join you on that tiny drink you have there?' Her voice was deep and husky. She laughed; her jaws unhinged as though she had no restrictions in her life.

He poured a glass for her promptly, and she sipped it. 'Ah, merci, is this not what the good Lord ordered?'

The gentlemen laughed lightly. Margaret adjusted her blouse, and rolled her sleeves.

Thomas passed a small envelope to Charles. While he opened it, he asked about the days' activities around the country.

'The Broken Hill boycott of the Queen's coronation last year was such a success that we have to emulate that level of organisation,' Thomas said.

'Yes, indeed. So, who has been assigned to lead the Ndola group for this one?'

'Lusaka is doing well. But here, we are all too exposed, Kombe. The police are hot on our trail. There have been too many arrests, and we are spending more time fundraising for the families of the incarcerated than we are on strategic planning. We need to change the approach for this one.

Tomorrow we need someone to go to the Polish butchery along Cecil Rhodes. Someone who they don't know or least expect. Someone fearless enough to enter the "Europeans only" door. Only then can our picketers come onto the scene.'

'Are we ready for it? Remember, this has to be peaceful. We have to select someone who is able to demonstrate great restraint. I don't know if a new person can manage that.'

'We have thought through it carefully, sir. It has to be a person who the public will endear to. And when I say public, I mean both non-whites and whites.'

'Who do you have in mind?'

Charles lay his article on its face. The group stopped what they were doing.

'Your wife, sir.'

'Me?' Margaret looked up from her badge sewing.

'Yes, you, but don't worry. Ms Fabiola will be there with you.'

'Fabiola? But she could get deported, right?'

'Yes, and you might get banished to some faraway village. In the best case scenario, back to Chinsali. But that won't happen. We have some strong lawyers from our empathisers. They have made sure that you will have a watertight defence should things escalate to that point.'

The toddler crawled out of his cot, reaching for his mother.

'Bana CJ, you will do this for your country, won't you?' Her husband's question bore into her while she felt her baby's soft hands stroking her leg. Her husband studied her face. There was silence in the room except for the voices of the men outside.

Margaret looked at the baby who was now climbing onto her lap. She looked at the NR trio – their eyes wide as saucepans.

Fabiola moved to sit next to Margaret and the baby.

She smelled of cinnamon. 'They have planned this very carefully. We can do it if we go over all the details tonight. Nothing will happen to your child, alright?' She looked at the group of ladies, prompting them with a slow nod, and they followed.

'We will be back home tomorrow. I promise.'

'But my English? I express myself better in Bemba.'

'Ah, but me too! I speak French, not English. We have scripts to practise for each scenario. If things get bad, I will sing in Lingala, and you can back me up in Bemba, eh?' She laughed again, this time her sparkling eyes looked straight into Margaret's. Margaret could not resist a shy chuckle.

*

The bunting along the glossy butchery flapped against its glass windows. There was no rain. The skies were a pleasant cloudless blue. Margaret looked at the reflection of herself next to Fabiola. The vinyl sign pasted across the top of the glass door was emblazoned with 'Europeans only'.

A white family whizzed past her like she was invisible. They strolled into the shop. Children half her age were allowed to go through a door that she could not. She thought of how, every Friday, she lined up to purchase a parcel of sticky, rotten meat from the small hole in the wall at the back of the butchery. She closed her eyes to remember the flies buzzing towards the pong from the parcels she and her neighbours came home with. She thought of all the Africans around the country who, in solidarity had said no to meat for the past few months. The vicious beatings and unnecessary imprisonment flooded her heart. In that moment, she felt deeply for all of them, as though each one of them were her son, CJ. She thought of the world which he would find if this law did not change.

Shiny medallions of pork were served to the family in the window. The shop owner came around from the counter and knelt to talk to one of the children. He showed them a chart of a bull demarcated and labelled at different parts of its body.

The children pointed at the shank and the rump. They livened up and licked their lips as the mother smiled proudly.

Garnishes of parsley shone green around the face of a dead pig. It smiled at Margaret from its bed of ice.

'Fabiola. It's time. Let's go inside!'

The two ladies held hands and walked into the shop. Its bell sounded, and its patrons reeled in disbelief.

'Read the sign on the door! You can get your meat like everybody else – from the hatch at the back on Friday!' the overweight butcher said as he rapped his fingers along the counter. They made a heavy gallop that echoed across the room.

'We would like a kilogram of chuck and two dressed chickens please. Like everybody else,' Fabiola said.

'You have to go through the back like all the Africans. It says clearly, "Europeans only".'

Margaret interjected. 'Yes, indeed, but I am a citizen of Northern Rhodesia, and unfortunately, the Federation. I deserve to be served the same goods and services as anyone else regardless of race, creed, or colour in any shop that I choose to enter. Please, can I have my order?'

Two stern faced men, who looked like the butcher may have many moons before, stepped out to flank him. Fabiola continued to say the lines as they had practiced.

'Sir, you are in violation of the United Nations Charter, Article 73. Can you promptly serve my friend and me, and we will be out of your way?'

'Get out! If you look at the sign below that one, it says "Reserve the right to entry". I am well within the law to ask you to leave peacefully.'

The ladies turned to look outside, and there was a line of smartly dressed picketers. Cameras snapped pictures. The ladies sat next to the European families who had resigned to being locked inside.

'We will wait until we are served. We have all day.'

They pulled out their yarns of wool and begun to knit. The pair of burly men came from around the counter and lifted the duo. They carried the women kicking and screaming into a cold room. The ladies were thrown to the cold floor. They sat up next to each other. Carcasses swung low in rows of pink, and the metallic sharpness of blood filled their nostrils. After the steel door shut tight and the room went dark, Margaret dissolved into tears.

'My son! My son! Why did I let Charles talk me into this? What's going to happen to CJ if we die in here?' Margaret banged on the door, on the walls, but they absorbed her actions – giving her silence in return. She flung her fists at the shadows of swinging beasts.

'I too had a son.' Fabiola said quietly. Her voice filled the room as she sung of a baby taken away from her, to a land far away. A baby who was neither white nor black, but both. Margaret froze. Her heart breaking with each note. She sat next to Fabiola, and they hummed together while they waited.

By the time the authorities arrived, the entrance of the shop was cloudy with tear gas and the dispersing crowd was trotting down the road. Police escorted the ladies out, bundling them into the back of a Land Rover.

*

Seven days after the event, Margaret arrived home with Charles. Fabiola was deported and banished for life from the Federation of Northern, Southern Rhodesia, and Nyasaland.

The sun would rise and set against the pawpaw tree outside. She let the position of its shadow guide her sense of time. She refused to let her baby go. She cuddled him day and night.

She would later stand in the crowd as Charles and Thomas closed the hatch with the Polish butcher. Brick by brick, the gentlemen layered the hole with wet cement until it existed no more. Until it became history. A story that would be told one day. The men shook hands in front of the cameras and signed documents with the chamber of commerce – and read their speeches.

At last, a basic human right was granted to Africans and all non-whites.

At last, they could enter any public shop with dignity.

At last, Fabiola was gone.

PART II

CHAPTER 15

MAGGIE OLUWASEUN AYOMIDE
LUSAKA, ZAMBIA, 2017

As I HURRY THROUGH my office corridors, creatives behind huge Macs each give me a thumbs-up while their eyes are glued to their screens, colossal earphones balancing on top of their heads. My heels serenade the floor – at times fast, and at others almost dragging.

'Hey, Ms. Maggie, are you OK? Maggie? Are you there?' One of the Wakanda-looking kids asks, his arms are festooned with artistic tattoos that led to a half-hour conversation when I first interviewed him. He imparted some enchanting words about how the success of the human race is connected to both its past and its present.

'A continuum of energies,' he said, and my attention was clutched tightly by the wavy, interlocking symbols glistening along his brown skin.

'Hi, I'm fine. Thanks. Just a lot to deal with before I leave,' I reply, flashing my Colgate smile.

'Coolies, boss. I hope you have a good one! I hear Lagos is dope, man! The artists coming out of there are mind blowing. It's like they're on creative steroids or something! And the wardrobes in those videos – don't get me started!'

'Yeah dope,' I reply awkwardly.

He saunters to his office. 'Please take a selfie with D'Banj for me!'

'Ha ha ha! Very funny!' I shuffle through papers in my filing cabinet.

I close my office door gently to sneak a peek at a photograph of my father's parents from the eighties. I remove the wooden box with the domed lid from my lockable cabinet. I run my palms over its carved designs before I open it. Beautiful, brown, dimple in cheek people – my grandmother with her exotic Jamaican accent, strong eyes, elegant repose, flecks of golden jewellery on her ears and around her neck. In my disintegrating baby album, she is featured in fabulous corset dresses, her luscious black hair cascading in curls beneath the net of her burgundy fascinator. My grandfather is coolness personified, ever smart in grey trousers and a small moustache, smoke pipe to his lip.

Tapping the rosewood desk in my office, I look at the blue and yellow ticket from RwandAir. It has my flight details from Lusaka to Lagos and an overnight stop in Kigali. A myriad of feelings overlaps in the cave of my belly. I close my eyes so that I can bask in the joy of this moment, but all I can see is my father's eyes the last time I ever saw him. I smell that scent of desperation like it was yesterday.

All through secondary school, I fantasised that he would show up one day. When Bupe came to my school, I was hopeful that her dad would be able to find him for me. That request was the beginning of terrible words exchanged between my mother and Uncle CJ. Uncle Kabaso, in the middle, tried to speak to them both, but that didn't work. I had to promise not to bring it up again.

I changed my focus to God, and so rose every morning, thankful for the chance that he might show up that day. I would practice how I would greet him, and this would change often. Sometimes it was a soft, wet reunion – other times it was a melodramatic showdown filled with rage. My new addiction to Nollywood fuelled my imagination.

Maybe I would be driving down the road in my large Rolls Royce, and we would lock eyes while he was selling ripe yellow bananas at the traffic lights, and I would stop to offer him a lift. I would roll my window down and look at him over my jet black Fendi sunglasses with a fabulous gele balancing at the top of my head. He would dust his face off and fall to his exposed knees asking for my forgiveness. My driver would chase away his paupers for friends, and I would save him. He would move into my glittering mansion and be forever grateful.

My fantasies ended last week when my phone flashed a strange number. It rang six times while I sat in a meeting with agriculture investors from Israel. When the meeting finally concluded, I stepped from the freezing cold boardroom and returned the call.

'Hello, I missed a call from this number?'

'Oluwaseun,' his voice purred through the phone. No one used my middle name, I rarely heard it uttered, yet here it was, rolling off his tongue three times like sweet molasses.

I stood in stunned silence.

'It's me.' he said.

'I know who it is. Hello.'

'I know this must be quite a shock. But I've been trying to reach you for ages now.'

Ages, he said. The word tumbled in my head until it lost meaning.

I wished he was surprised at the silence from my end, but he wasn't. He rambled on about how long it has been and how it would be nice to see me. He told me that my grandparents were elderly now and that they were begging him every single day, asking for me to go to Lagos. He mentioned a woman named Charleen numerous times. 'Charleen and the boys,' he kept saying like it was one word. Something like the holy trinity. Something I was supposed to be familiar with. 'They won't be in Lagos this time, but they would love to meet you soon.'

'So, are you coming?' he asked again as my silence lingered.

'When?' I managed.

'Next week if you can.'

'Of course!' I jerked awkwardly, as I watched the traffic below from the top floor of the InterContinental. I should have been more nonchalant, in less of a hurry, but I wasn't. My heart was beating so fast, I could feel it through my skin. I didn't feel the magic I had prepared for. Instead, I felt my breakfast bubble up. I ended the call and sprinted into a bathroom before anyone could see me. I let my insides out until I was gasping for air. Images of him and 'Charleen and the boys' beam like a projected film before me.

*

I peruse through my calendar and count back the days to my last period. It doesn't look good. I am going to start a family with my husband, but it is impossible to turn a new page when I don't know what was on the last one. Hopefully, Lagos will have answers for me.

The mere thought of Lagos, or of my grandparents, has always been a display of disloyalty to mother, which in her world is equivalent to medieval era treason. I dial her line again, in vain, and I meet with a recorded voice, the same one I've heard since I told her I was leaving: The number you have dialled is not in use. Please try again later.

She has not spoken to me since I gave her the news.

'He's going to leave you, the way he left us before, Maggie. If you love your life, you will stay here.'

'But, Mum, he is my father. And you've never explained why you divorced in the first place. I don't need your permission anymore. I will see my father and my people – before they – before they are no longer alive.'

'Do you remember seeing the headline cut-out about the Wall Street Crash? Your father was so selfish, and greedy, and stupid. He put everything the family had without any of our consent, and we lost everything!'

'He is still my father, Mum. And you should have let me see him. You push everyone away, even Uncle CJ. I'm not doing this with you anymore.'

'If you go, Maggie, you are no longer a daughter of mine. Do you understand?'

*

With a heavy sigh, I peel myself away from my desk and leave my office so I can prepare for my early morning journey. I look at my watch, 6.15 p.m. I still tell the time in a 12-hour format. Ideally, I should say 18.15 hours like a proper Zambian woman – as I have been taught to. It is dark outside. As usual, I am the last one to leave. I switch off the lights at my small firm and punch in the code for the alarm. Isn't it ironic that I do country marketing for a living, and I have not been to my own since I was a child?

The drive home is slow. No traffic. No drama. I deliberately drive at 40 kilometres per hour, taking a longer route than usual. The hooters behind me are drowned by Anita Baker's voice on my stereo. At the traffic lights, our local aspiring cross country runner with his own version of dreadlocks is dressed in full athletic gear. He folds his body in half to touch his toes, and he stretches upwards to take deep breaths. His swimming goggles will serve him well because there are light showers. Today, I don't mind that he will outrun my car.

I drive past him and find my way home.

There, I wait for the electric gate to open. My indicator flashes, and my windscreen is kept visible by the timely rubber screech of wipers. I check my rearview mirror to be sure that I have not been followed, a nightly ritual.

The modern decor on my black iron gate moves noisily to the left, and it reveals an empty two-port garage. Lights off. There is no life here. I fill up my gaping suitcase. Neatly pressed clothes folded perfectly over each other, each line according to colour, black, pink, orange, red. Shoes for any potential event: heels, sandals, sneakers and boots. I have three books to read and presents for my grandparents. Antihistamines, vitamin C, and sunblock. Passport, credit card, some dollars. I think I'm good to go. Terrence, my husband, is still not back yet, even though I will be gone for a week.

I look for the notebook with our suitcase key combinations, and I find scribbled notes from our premarital church lessons. In there, I stop at the page that has a drawing of a basic house. The 'House of Love' the visiting pastor from Minnesota had called it. The foundation is carefully marked: Agape, Godly Love. The trunk: Philia, Brotherly Love. The roof: Eros, Sexual Love. He proclaimed this revelation to a room of us, eager endorphin-high twenty-somethings, that this is all we needed to build a solid marriage. I run my fingers over the one dimensional stick house repeatedly.

The large hand of the clock on my bedside makes loud, steady ticks.

In the middle of the night, Terrence creeps into our room. The squeaking of his sneakers on the tiled floor gives him away. He stops to take them off. He changes his clothes with the help of his phone light. He bumps into everything. He climbs into bed gently. I toss and I turn. Anguish knots a tight ball in the pit of my stomach. Each of us face the wall of our bedside, a gulf between us large enough for Moses and the freed slaves to walk through casually without worry of it closing.

The tick of the clock remains constant.

His breathing is shallow and fast. My heart rate increases, and my breaths join his.

'Babe, I'm not going to ask you where you've been because

I'm past that at this point. But, tell me – is this what we have come to?' I ask, still facing my wall.

'I don't know.' The scent of whisky mixed with a new cologne makes me move further to the edge of the bed. It makes me queasy. 'It seems we have, madam boss, queen of queens, Miss I-don't-listen-to-anyone-but-me,' he retorts, tugging at the duvet.

'That's not fair!'

'Oh really?' he asks. 'Is taking the pill in secret fair?'

His words fall right where he intended for them to. I am crushed and defeated, and I imagine a satisfied smirk across his face. Yes, it is true. I started taking the pill when he wanted to have a child, but I stopped when I saw how much it was killing us. He hasn't let it go since he found out, and now I am punished every day, even though I may be carrying his baby. I don't think there is any point in telling him yet. I don't know if I want to keep it, and many days, I don't know if I want to be in this marriage.

We agree to use the time during this one week apart to think about what we are going to do with our relationship. The funny thing is I still do not know what has led us here. It is complex, this sticky emotional spiderweb we are trapped in. Two years of a fine balancing act – each one on his silk line, wondering who will fall first.

The silence in our room is loud. Ear splitting. I want to hide in my bunker and not be here. To turn on a TV and curl up with my favourite blanket. I want warm fluffy socks and a hot cup of cocoa. I want to be in bed, eating tuck at midnight like we did in boarding school with my cousin Bupe, the only person who really gets me. Actually, both her and Grandpa Charles. I want to feel that feeling of belonging again. I hope I will find something close enough to this in Lagos.

I get out of bed to look back at him snoring without a care in the world. I slip into my study, and I dial Bupe. I need to hear her voice.

CHAPTER 16

BUPE KOMBE
LONDON, UK, 2017

'WASTEMAN! HE'S A CERTIFIABLE wasteman, and he's going to take you down with him!' Those are the last words my mum spat at me the last time we spoke. I screamed back and told her I never want to see her again. But now, I need her.

I hang up the phone after a long chat with Maggie, and I can't help but look around my matchbox of a bedsit. Could Mum have been right? Have I really thrown my life away? Jerome hammocks in the sunken sofa, focused on his video game. His golden Cuban links around his neck clink against each other, and the smoke from his bong fills the air. His jewellery seems perversely expensive in our little home. His trainers are stacked high, above his safe, which costs more than everything I own. It sits camouflaged by our clothes in the wardrobe – the contents of which, I prefer not to ask. He splatters advancing soldiers into squirts of blood on the telly.

His bong stands on a square table next to him.

I open the fridge for a beer. I need to absorb what my cousin has told me. Her dad's come back out of nowhere, like the living dead. Just like that, he's handing her some mystical olive branch, looking for a grand reunion. I can't believe it, and if I can't, I can only imagine what Aunty Stella must be thinking.

Maggie asked me once, when we were kids, to see if my dad could find him. My dad was fine with it, but he was tremendously apprehensive about how his sister would react, so he suggested it to her in one of his red enveloped letters, and she blew her top. My mum tried to call her and speak with her, but even she felt the wrath of my aunt. It was settled after that. No one was to interfere in her matters or anything to do with Maggie and Uncle Abisola.

Maggie's done phenomenally well in my books. She started a firm all by herself, and it's taken her around the world. She met Terrence after university and married him a couple of years ago. '*Terrence.* What kind of name is that for a Zambian bloke?' my mother had said, and we laughed.

I think she married him because he comes from a large family. One with aunties and uncles, grandmothers and grandfathers, people who pop in unannounced and can't wait for you to give them children to play with. The kind that has family meetings because you've decided to change the colour of your socks. The kind who fight on occasion, but always kiss and make up. Families who meet every year in matching t-shirts, who begin their meals seated in the same sequence unless there has been a death or birth. That's what I think Maggie married, not necessarily him. But now that she has it, what she's always wanted, I'm not quite sure she has a clue of what to do with it.

In the morning, I agree to meet my mother at Brockwell Park. She's only coming because I told her about Maggie and her dad. She's laid a plaid blanket on the grass, and she has a bucket of Morley's chicken. She knows it's my favourite.

'How you doing, kid? How's your new job?'

She knows the answer, so I don't know why she's asking me such a stupid question.

'It wasn't my fault. I was late because the Victoria line got cancelled after I waited a whole hour. It always does! And you know this already.'

'Hmm,' she answers, looking at me intently. 'You're going to have to choose what you want to do one day, Bupe. Living like this is way beneath your potential. Is it something we did? Is it me?'

I sigh. 'No, Mum.'

'So, where has the fight in you gone?'

'Not everyone lives for battle.' We keep quiet for some time and she offers me the crunchy drumsticks.

'I wonder why Abisola is back. Like why now? Did your cousin tell you anything else?'

I shake my head slowly while I watch a man in the distance get down on one knee and propose to his girl.

She continues. 'I met him when we were 16 years old in 1967. His parents lived a lavish life here – their parties were lively, and his dad knew everyone. His mum, Merlene, she gave your nan a job as a cook, and she paid her well. That's how we were able to save up for the Curry House.'

'What was he like?'

'Abisola? He was a nice kid, very cheeky, able to get his way with anyone, a tad spoilt I'm afraid. He was extremely intelligent and would turn into whatever his environment needed him to.' She's laughing now, at a memory.

'A bit like a chameleon?'

She laughs and nods her head. 'Yes, I suppose you could say that!'

She throws her head back and lets out a sigh. 'He asked me to join him and your dad for a dinner party at the house. I knew your dad liked me, but he was just so shy, so Abs made the first move for him.'

'How did Aunty Stella leave him? I know they went to Zambia suddenly, but why?'

'You've heard of Black Monday? After a long run the stock market in New York crashed. Well, Abs was a bit of a greedy cow, but in all fairness, he was pretty smart, so he thought he could earn some money on the stock exchange.'

'So, did he?'

'Unfortunately, yes, he did, at first. But he did it against equity on their Marble Arch home, the one your nan has shown you since you were a kid. The family lost the house, and all of a sudden, they were owing a lot of big people a lot of big money. Abs vanished. Your aunt and Maggie had to leave town one night, and that was that really.'

'He left them to face the heat alone? What a twat!'

'Language, miss.'

'No wonder Aunty Stella is so bitter. Do you think we can trust him this time?'

'Look, I think this is an opportunity for Maggie. Maybe she can finally have some closure, or even enjoy her dad for the rest of her life. But, knowing the guy I once knew, I would keep one eye open. You never know with Abisola Ayomide.'

'Now, that was a wasteman move.'

'Yes, it was. Aunty Stella got out. When will you?' The lines in her forehead make tunnels as her eyebrows lift.

I turn to look at the lady who's now jumping and kissing the man who's proposed. She makes him stand, and they ask someone to take a photo of them.

'How did Dad propose to you?' I ask her this all the time. She loves to tell me.

'It was after the riots, and your nan was nursing me. I hadn't spoken a word for a whole week. I was in her room, and she was feeding me a bowl of hot corn soup. Daddy came in donning a curly afro wig, and he recited Una Marson in a terrible Jamaican accent.

> I like me black face,
> And me kinky hair,
> But nobody loves dem
> … What won't a man go

Some kind of girl to win.
Your mama loves you
And your colour is high.'

She's laughing now. 'And I said to him, "Yes, CJ, me love your black face, an' your kinky hair! I will definitely marry you!"'

CHAPTER 17

MAGGIE OLUWASEUN AYOMIDE
LAGOS, NIGERIA, 2017

THE PASSENGERS MAKE A beeline for the double decker RwandAir airbus and the queue curves along the grey tarmac. Once on the plane, they fill each seat – not one space empty. Nigerians on their way to Lagos from verdant, police filled, highly organised Kigali. People have a sense of urgency as they proceed to their seats, no mercy for the lanky man who takes a luxurious walk in the aisles looking for cabinet space for his hand luggage.

'Dis year I beg, move oh!' they all say in a chorus.

I take my seat next to a young man who has a face full of scarification. Lines on his forehead, his cheeks, and his chin, all at an angle like upside down V's. He greets me and tells me he is Nupe – a student from Nigeria living in Uganda. He asks me where I am from, and I hesitate.

A trio of women sit in the row behind us. From the conversation, I can tell that they are on their way from Lusaka to Lagos for miracle prayers at TB Joshua Ministries.

The lady in the middle seat is sweating and weak. The other two repeatedly prop her up as she slumps to the floor with fatigue. One lady fastens her seat belt for her and tries to wipe her brow and fan her at the same time. They are speaking loudly, clicking their fingers in the air, asking God to bind all principalities and forces of darkness. They shout, 'Shatamalata kata brakata rakata rakata rakata! God cover the pilot and his crew in the blood of Jesus, clear the way for them, so that your servant here can be healed by your hand, Ropheka! Give her strength to reach her miracle land for healing.' I look back at the Nupe boy and decide not to reveal my Zambian identity.

The entire aircraft promptly goes to sleep, completely wrapped in blankets like human cordon bleu, revealing only the tops of their hairstyles and the soles of their feet. I close my eyes and try to remember them.

Memories of a gentle grandmother come fleetingly. We would sit on the fluffy carpet where she would braid my hair in loose cornrows for bedtime. The smell of coconut and shea butter wafted from her soft, cool hands as they danced along the neatly made lines running down my head. The Manhattans in white jumpsuits on the telly singing something about kissing and saying goodbye. Me asking where my mother was and why I could only speak to her over the static of the phone once a week. My grandmother would go around the subject in a way that left me puzzled.

'Do you know why I like to braid your hair in cornrows, darling?'

'So, it's soft in the morning?'

'Well, yes, honey. But, more importantly, because we should never forget.'

'Forget what, Grandma?'

'That we did all the hard work.'

'I don't get it, Grandma.'

'This hair style reminds us of the cornfields. Of the plantations – corn, cotton, and sugar. My people's people's people – they had to work the sugar plantations all day in the scorching sun. Cornrows are a style that kept our hair kempt while we worked. It crowned our heads like the kings and queens we are, despite being reduced to less than human.'

At that, I sit upright from my slouch, push my shoulders back, lift my chin, and cross my legs.

'To make a cornrow, you need all of the hair to join in neatly, row by row – and that's how we worked – together. It also means, my darling, we all need each other, and it's the same for our family. Don't worry, your mother will be home soon.'

My grandfather was never with us physically – at least I don't remember him there. Not the touch of him nor the smell of him like I did my grandmother. But I remember the story of him – of his presence, his charismatic personality of how gregarious he was. The big man around town, the host of London's best parties. He now remains a figure in a picture frame laughing with friends, whisky in hand, good looks, and comfort surrounding him.

Finally, we descend, and as the plane falls, my emotions swell and mount. Something opens my entire being like a floodgate. I weep as though someone has died. The feeling is raw, open, cavernous, engulfing. How can the return to a land you barely know be so gripping? The poor Nupe boy is uncomfortable, not knowing which way to look. His scars turn upwards in worry – he offers me a tissue.

We touch down, and I pray for the land of my ancestors to be good to me. That my father will be there and that I will find favour in the eyes of my grandparents. That they will tell me more, help me understand my lineage better. That they will embrace me like they once did. That this void in my heart will finally be filled.

The hostess tells everyone to leave their blankets behind – there is zero adherence to her plea.

At the luggage carousel, I stand next to a gentleman who has just come off the same flight. His shirt announces loudly across his chest that it is '100% Genuine Dolce & Gabbana.'

I wonder what it would be if it were anything less than the declared percentage. His belt is tight around his waistline, like he's been struck by the curse of prosperity.

'I saw you in Rwanda,' he says in a matter of fact voice, like one who is used to being an authority on any subject.

'Oh, I see,' I respond.

He persists. 'Pardon me, but is that ring real?' He points at my marriage band.

I nod warily.

'I think we separated when I went into first class. Me sef, I was coming from Dubai. The first class in that Rwanda plane is actually impressive. You can evun lie down on flatbed.' I laugh.

The carousel makes complete passes a few times, but our luggage does not reveal itself. He seems to lose his composure.

'This is ridiculous! First class in Dubai doesn't treat you like this. First class anywhere else in the world will ensure that they release your baggage first!' He wipes his brow in frustration. He shifts his weight onto his other leg. 'Is this your first time in Nigeria?' he asks me.

'As an adult, yes, it is,' I say.

'Oho, where will you be staying?'

'Ikeja.'

'Oh, I see.' He reaches for his business card and hands one to me. It reads in gold foil: Bola Richards. Not disguising his disappointment, he carries on. 'Me sef, I live in Lekki. It's on Victoria Island. Life there is much better than on the mainland. Please get in touch. Perhaps I can show you the country club where I play golf.'

Thankfully, his bag arrives, and he walks away flustered, probably wondering how I could pass up such a chance. My bag arrives shortly, and I grab it off the carousel.

My moment of truth arrives. The one I have been imagining all my life, and now I feel weak with anxiety. What if my father isn't here to meet me?

'Hmmm, madam, ooh!' the passing trolley guy says to me.
I turn around, surprised.

'What is ya name?'

'Maggie.'

'Diaris somtin about you, actually – everytin' about you. De way you walk, de way you talk, and evun ya name iz beautiful! Diarias a God oh!' He rolls his eyes pretending to look skywards, as if his prayer had been answered.

I laugh at his boldness. There is no way that would happen in Lusaka. 'Well, hello, Lagos!'

At the small window, I change Dollars into Naira. A strong aura and a familiar voice, creep up from behind me. 'Maggie?' I turn, and it is my loving uncle Tayo.

His hair is worn in long silver dreadlocks secured in a ponytail. He is so skinny; his shoulders jut out of the sleeves of his traditional shirt. His fingernails are brown, like his skin. He is visibly excited; we smile at each other – both unsure where to start.

After a brisk hug but a warm welcome, and an uncomfortable laugh, he escorts me outside. He dramatically chases the trolley boy and walks me outside to arrivals. There stands my father; rounder and fuller than he once was. Laughing eyes behind his glasses. My own, red and puffy, tired from the long night of tears and the flight.

'Maggie, my baby,' he says.

'Daddy.'

We embrace. Strangely, it feels as natural as something we do every day.

We all head to the pickup area, teeming with people of various shapes and sizes. The midday sun sits right above us, hot and low, the air enclosing, constricting like a four-sided cage. A policeman, possibly an army man, approaches and makes jest with my father. His arms are so long, right down to his knees. His hands look murderous, extraordinarily large and turned inwards. His red beret and black uniform are scary, but his laugh is warm and syrupy.

We get into an old Jeep, and the hot leather receives us. The aircon is broken, and we drive away from Murtala Muhammed International Airport onto the highway. My father shows me the cantonment area in Ikeja where Uncle Tayo's family lived – they talk about the great parties they would have there during his summer holidays. On the mainland, a crisscross of electric lines sag and hang low from the many poles. The greyish smog like air sits close, and my father says it has something to do with Lagos being at sea level. I don't believe him.

The sound of pressed hooters is persistent, with only short bursts of silence between. A droptop Bentley materialises, as though out of a hip-hop video, with a man in Medusa sunglasses and a thick beard. He has a woman with beige skin in the passenger side. The street hawkers try to jump into his back seat while they admire the big oga. A younger one almost succeeds.

'Woz wrong with you now? U dey craze?' His big beard moved along with his words.

'Oga, you go buy cold water?' They try to appease him.

'You wan die? Dem dey follow you from house, if u no comot from hia I go slap you!' He makes a move for his glove compartment, and they scatter away. He curses them—their mothers, and their children, and their children's children.

I look around in wonder. Okadas and three-wheelers zoom past us. Danfos carting their passengers blare a cacophony of Drake and Davido. Their conductors hang out of the doors of the moving motors – defiant to death. Passengers jump on and off the buses without the vehicles coming to a complete stop. Bank brands are lined up everywhere, shouting for attention, orange GT Bank, blue Ecobank, red United Bank for Africa.

*

Finally, we turn off the main highway and onto a slip road, followed by the sound of the Imam calling all brethren to prayer. The bumpy dust road boasts suya roasts packed into newspaper funnels. The tomato grinder down the road puts his onion, garlic, tomato, and bell peppers into his welded funnel and turns the wheel while his liquid gold pours into waiting yellow buckets below. His crotched singlet and wrapper are a befitting outfit for the heat and the work on which he concentrates single mindedly. His customers line up, ready to collect their pre-mix for tonight's stews.

My father explains that the grinder has lived opposite them for many years and that his tomato grinding business has sent all his children to school abroad. The grinder's wife disappears into their home behind a lilac-coloured curtain at the main door entrance. Right next to them stands an opulent mansion completely fenced in with barbed wire carefully placed along its perimeter. The house occupies its entire floor space, so it almost touches the barbed wall. It towers above its humble neighbour, pointing forwards as if to say, 'Judge not,' but rather to look the opposite direction, at what I will come to find is our own duplex.

The gate is opened by a skinny man-cub with fuzz for a moustache. He can't be over 15. Ironically, his name is Youngharry. But then I remember that it is not uncommon to have teenage workers in this part of Africa. The squeaking sound of hot stones against rubber announces our arrival into the compound.

At last, the sound of angry car horns is no more. There is a different noise here. Generators, televisions, faceless voices haggling. We go upstairs to my grandparents' room.

There they are. Here they are.

Alive, breathing, in full colour, seated side by side on their bed, dressed exquisitely to go nowhere. Him, in a crisp safari suit; her in a golden ankara boubou.

Again, I cry. The sight of my grandmother is overbearing. I kneel next to her, and she says softly and slowly, 'Maggie is crying. I never thought I would see you again in this lifetime.'

My grandfather looks baffled. He opens up his palms to demand an explanation while his mouth hangs open in shock.

'Ehn? What's going on here? Who is this lady?' He laughs naughtily.

'Daddy, this is Maggie, your first granddaughter. She has come home,' my father announces triumphantly.

'Maggie?' It confuses him. 'Whose child is that?'

'Mine, Daddy.'

My grandmother is a husk of her former self now. Her Jamaican vowels and consonants are rounded and laboured in effort to explain to her best friend that 'it's Abisola's guurl.'

'Abisola?'

'Yes. Abisola. You don't know Abs? He's right here.'

I offer quietly, 'Oluwaseun.'

'Oluwaseun?!' His eyes light up. 'Is it you? That is your tribal name. You have come back?'

'Yes, Grandpa.'

'Oh, we thank God! Do you know what your name means? It means, I thank my living God!'

He speaks with such conviction that he clasps my hands, and I kneel before him at the foot of his bed. He is fair in complexion, his face oval with angles at the cheekbones, freckles sprinkled generously across his nose. His eyes are searching my face – a circle of blue halos around his brown pupils. His long nose bridges to his mouth giving way to a twitching bottom lip with a middle gap in the lower set of teeth. He asks after my mother and asks where she is.

He smiles all the time and laughs at his own jokes. My grandmother rolls her eyes to dismiss his naughtiness with both familiarity and sarcasm.

'And your uncle CJ? Is he still in London with your aunt Jasmine?' she asks.

'Yes, he is, Ma.'

'How are they?'

'They are fine, Grandma. I speak to Bupe, their daughter, all the time!'

'I wonder where her grandmother is. She used to look after us in London – best cook I ever had.'

'From what I hear, she has moved back to Jamaica.'

'Lucky her! England is not the same for people like us anymore. When we were needed, they told us we could stay as long as we wanted. But they keep on changing the rules, you see. Now people like me there can't even get the NHS to look at them. More than half a century since we got there, and they still treat us like bald headed step chil'un!'

I nod my head in agreement and look at my shoes like a five year old in the London playground.

'Relax, dear, have a bath. Feel at home –' Grandmother says. Before she can finish, my grandfather stands up like a school teacher, coming to life with anecdotal advice.

'When a cock goes to a new town, it stands on one foot in case everyone there forbids it to walk on two! Please, put your other foot down my child and walk!' He laughs and a smiling nurse turns to Grandma.

She instructs her to fix me a bath. It's more a bucket of warm water in the shower as the taps don't run. I am shown to my bedroom, which, like in the films, has no duvet or blankets, just white, blue speckled cotton sheets placed carefully on a double bed with a fan in the corner. An old painting of my grandfather from his younger days sits on the floor as though waiting for its destination – hopefully to be hung on a wall once more. As though to complete the frame of my Naija movie scene, I hear a keyboard and traditional flute emanating from the neighbours' thunderous surround system. They are watching a local film. The closeness of the buildings is something I am not used to – I follow the plot in two minutes and let the drama unfold. It sounds like a love triangle between a pauper, a rich prince, and a beautiful village girl.

'I'm home!' I laugh. Finally.

*

The next morning, we cross each other's paths along the corridor.

'Good morning, Grandpa!'

'Good morning, madam. I hope you are well,' he replies curtly.

'Yes, Grandpa, I am.'

He walks away with a confused frown, shaking his head. In his bedroom, he asks his wife who the new visitor is.

The introduction begins once more.

He remembers again.

He animates.

We do this repeatedly throughout the day. I enjoy it because I get to meet him again and again for all the years lost.

CHAPTER 18

MAGGIE OLUWASEUN AYOMIDE
LAGOS, NIGERIA, 2017

SOAKING IN MY OWN sweat, I wake to the sound of generators turning on along our street. A grumble strong enough to shake my slender body prompts a quick walk to the bathroom. I let my tummy run from the delicious white pepper soup I had the night before.

Once done, I prepare to wash my hands with some sweet smelling hand wash. 'Hmm,' I think, 'this is nice!' I pick it up to register the brand, and to my alarm, it is well labelled with a picture of a dead man. He has a hefty grey beard and he wears blue agbada. The label says: Thank you for attending the funeral of Professor, Doctor, Chief Kola Adesina MBA, FCCA. May God richly bless you. I throw it back but laugh at myself all the way back down the corridor as I head towards my grandparents.

Grandmother is there, as always, beautiful and elegant, her coconut water next to her, fan blowing through her silver hair. Grandad is holding her hand, telling her another joke which she pretends to hear for the first time.

'Grandma, do you mind today if I ask questions about where you and Grandpa are from?'

'Of course not, darling. Sit and get comfortable.'

'Uh!' Grandpa protests.

'When two trees fall on each other, you start by removing the top one.' He laughs.

'Therefore, it is me who will start.'

She rolls her eyes again but smiles at me. 'Do you know my mother was Esan – from Ekpoma? Your great grandmother. My father, your great grandfather, was Yoruba, Eko – Lagos bloodline through and through. Your great grandmother was a strong woman who made a small fortune in agriculture. She met your great grandfather when she had already established a farm with her bare hands and a small piece of land, which her father had left for her. I am telling you this so you know you are from hardworking stock, my girl.'

Grandpa turns to face Grandma. 'This woman sitting next to me – this fine woman from across the ocean – if it were not for her, I would not have made all the investments that made our family comfortable. Even after a mighty fall, we were still comfortable enough to have some of our own assets. I am nothing without her.'

My grandmother blushes. He strokes her hand. My body tenses as I watch them. It makes me uncomfortable when it should make me happy.

'How is your husband, Maggie? Can you bring me some pictures?' she asks.

'Of course, Ma.' I fumble through my phone.

'Here you go.' I show her studio photos of my husband and me – perfect poses for the camera. Makeup flawless. Outfits matching. Smiles like four-year-olds with smooth milk teeth. Happiness – a visual facade.

'He is a fine young man. When do you plan on having children?' She giggles naughtily.

I jump into my PR suit and give my well-practiced answer. 'When the time is right, Grandma. I've had so much work on my plate and so has he – and I guess it hasn't happened yet.'

'Ehen!' Grandpa chimes in.

'Do you know a snake has no tummy an' yet he looks for space to put intestines? Tell that husband of yours to get serious!'

'Jacob!' Grandma gives him an admonishing look.

He turns his lips upside down and claps the back of his hand onto the palm of the other. 'But iz true oh!'

'I see, darling,' she says to me. 'Make sure you grow your home into something your heart will be eternally proud of.'

'Yes, ma'am.'

'OK, pele,' he puts his hands together. 'Kadan, kadan – gradual by gradual.' He looks to his wife for approval.

She asks me to come closer to her. I walk to her bed. As per my Bemba tradition, I kneel next to her. She grabs my hand firmly and pulls me in. 'There is something I need to say to you, Maggie. Your grandfather and I are in the late night of our lives – to say evening would be wishful thinking.' She laughs.

'It's taken so long to see you again, and if I don't say this now, I may never get the chance.' I look at her intently as she keeps her eyes on mine.

'I want you to know, in all that you do, no matter what, you are Ayomide! The first of the first.'

'Yes, Grandma,' I say – grateful for the words that take shape in my heart. A verbal coronation, a crown put to my head, a sense of restoration taking place. I take my seat on the throne that she placed in me many years ago. It is the mantle I have been searching for all my life – done in seconds with two sentences and the sincerity of a loving grandmother's eyes.

'Grandma, how did you end up in England, all the way from Jamaica in the 1950s? That was a very long time ago.'

'I know, my guurl. Tings was different in those days. Eat your egusi, an' I tell you the story.'

It feels strange to have another woman stroke my hand. Bupe is the only person in the world who has come so close – well, Terrence too, if you count men. At first, I am tense, watching the gnarled knuckles and misshapen fingers of my grandmother run up and down my arm. I want to disappear into them and see a time before mine, the sequence of events that led to this moment. Her calm energy finds its way in, settling my spirit through each touch – 'a continuum', the kid from my office called it.

Her nurse goes downstairs to return with a barefooted Youngharry who carries a tray of fufu and chicken egusi. They bring water to wash my hands, and I thank them. She curtsies and asks Youngharry to bring fried dodo for Grandma. I take my seat next to their bed and prepare myself for this historical ride I have been yearning for.

I let the yellowish green paste squish between my fingers, and the taste of melon seed with chicken bursts in my mouth. The fufu sticks to the roof of my mouth, its bland fluffiness taming the wild flavours in my soup.

She looks to see that I am enjoying it, and seeming satisfied, she reduces the volume on the television. All I hear is the sound of the fan, the chewing from my mouth, haggling voices, and squeaking brakes from outside. Grandpa and I look at her, ready for the tale.

'I went to England by sea – in the summer of 1948 – right after the war. I was a young teaching student and the adverts on the radio made England look like heaven, a place for a new life and a great career. They raised us to believe we were English too you know, part of the Commonwealth and subjects of the King.

In them days, it took at least a month on the horrid water. Never stable, always making one sway, especially when the weather was bad. I came from the most beautiful part of Jamaica – with sharp blue waters and plenty resorts – Runaway Bay.'

'Why is it called Runaway Bay if it's so beautiful?' I ask between mouthfuls of egusi.

'It has a whole world of underground caves with complex tunnels that run for miles. The slaves who used to escape from their masters would hide in there before they left the island. There was plenty of stories about pirates, too, using it to regroup before they set sail for Cuba.'

'So, you ran away from Runaway Bay?' I say.

She smiles back at me. 'I see you take after your grandfather.'

'Did you travel alone? Weren't you terrified?' I ask.

'I missed my grandmother sorely. I was not terrified. I was excited! But every single day I was on that ship, I wondered how she was. Whenever it got scary or felt like forever, I would go into my heart and imagine what my family was doing.'

'First, I knew it was hot. My grandfather would have finished another day of farming in the fields. My uncle would return from the water, smelling like sweat and gutted fish. His fingers were rough and rugged, but his heart kind and pure. Grandmother, your great grandmother, would put a special balm on his blistered hands made rough by the fish nets. They most likely would be together on the porch, listening to Grandfather on his fiddle.

'My grandmother, she used to shell baskets of peas, which would have nasty little worms come out of them, so one had to be careful of those. I tell you, child, the dark sea storms on that journey made me wish I was there with her, getting worms in my ears instead.' She laughs.

I sip my Maltina, allowing the bubbles to fizzle in my mouth. 'Go on, Grandma. Tell me more.'

'After so many weeks, at last we came in view of London. The Englishman on the television had called it the "Jamaicans El Dorado". We ran across the deck to watch the city become larger and larger with each minute. It felt like a dream come true! In retrospect, Jamaica was the Englishman's El Dorado!' She sucked on her teeth. 'We're the ones with the sunshine and the sugar, bananas, coconuts and heavenly beaches, but, I digress.'

'When we finally arrived, they gave us instruction to disembark the ship, and it felt like forever. I could not see because I was so short. Everyone was taller than me. Grown men and women shoved each other to get out first. A few steely eyed men in raincoats and hats kept shouting 'Order! Order, please! We are all going to get off, so can you please restrain yourselves, or we will have to do it for you!'

We felt the push from the crowd and moved forwards into

the weak sun and stinging wind. A lady in front of me had her legs buckle as she stepped onto the gangplank. After one month at sea, her legs were melted wax. She slipped sideways along the gangplank while she was covering her face from the cold wind with her large bag from the Kingston straw market. White men with cameras snapped pictures furiously, it was a terrible greeting I tell you.

'"36 Somerleyton Road, Lambeth. 36 Somerleyton Road, Lambeth" I whispered over and over under my breath. We had to show a little bespectacled man at a small table our passes and affidavits from the Justice of the Peace in Jamaica.'

'What were those?'

'They were papers we got from the courts before we left, to show that we were citizens of good standing,' she says. 'I was just so thankful that I had somewhere to go! Many others coming off the ship had to think of the cold first, and second, they had come intending to apply for work through the Labour Exchange Office. Some people had to stay in the underground train stations because that's where it was dry and warm.'

Grandfather interrupts the discussion.

'Just jump to the part where you bumped into this dashing young Naija boy oh!'

She blushes, pushing her hair behind her ears like a teenager. 'Now your grandfather, when he came into my life, he was like a ray of sunshine in the middle of long dark days. He was not tall; he was dapper. Hair cut close in the sides and back. In the front stood a tall coif shaped like a table. His suits tailored perfectly and his ties so flamboyant they defied the wet weather. His scent of confidence overpowered his cologne; it seeped everywhere! No one could say no to him.' We laugh.

'Whenever he walked me to my front door, he would tell me I would be a queen when he took me home to Nigeria.'

He laughs loud. 'Is that not what I did?'

'Now, you know in our days, in our minds, Africa was taboo! A thick, dark jungle, full of human sacrifice rituals and all that obeah nonsense, unless you were a Garveyist. Ain't no way I would have come all the way from Jamaica to England, to be taken all the way to some faraway place in Africa!'

We all laugh until she has tears in her eyes.

'But – the thought of being returned – prodigal; a queen – when all your life you know you are the descendant of slavery, of a stolen generation of Africans taken against their will from the same coast that this man wanted to take me – now, that was the romance in the romance, if you know what I mean?'

She holds his hand. He laughs. 'Obo aria ole are kin oria bhi agbon! Do you know what that means?'

I shake my head. Grandmother mouths along with him.

'Only your personal struggle can carve the way to your prosperity.' They nod in unison, and the room is quiet for a while.

'And so, we got married, and we had your dad only three years after my arrival in London.'

'Wow, thank you, Grandma. So, you two will be celebrating your 67th anniversary next year? That is amazing. Grandpa, you said your mother was Esan. What does that mean?'

'Esan, means the "ones who fled".' He threw his hands up in the air like he had just given the answer to a NASA problem.

'Fled what?' I ask quizzically.

'We fled one strict Oba in Benin and ran through the forests so we could make love and babies and play music while drinking to it – freely.' He chuckled.

'Esanomics now we like good things, oh!' he said, pointing at Grandma like it was supposed to be a secret signal.

We laugh again.

'Don't mind your grandfather. I'll give you some books to take home with you, my darling. Have a read so that you know where you come from.'

'Thank you, Grandma.' My core warms and sheer joy radiates all over my being. I don't understand what the knots in my belly are saying, but I look at the two of them and know this is what I want.

I ask Grandma if I can braid her hair and it delights her. We pull out the coconut butter, the fisted afro comb, and it is finally my turn to make cornrows in her hair.

'Do you miss Jamaica?'

'With all my heart; all of it.'

'And you will never go back?'

'Baby girl, I can barely walk. Imagine me on a flight halfway around the world. I wouldn't get there alive. I would be a BID – brought in dead!' She cackles. 'Besides, where your grandpa go, I go. But, if you can ever go there, visit Runaway Bay and blow sand into the ocean for me.'

'I will, Grandma.'

She goes quiet. 'My only regret is missing our Independence Day, having to watch it on television from so far away; who knows, maybe I would have married Alexander Bustamante! He was such a handsome man! I bet Princess Margaret had a hard time signing all those formal papers, giving away that beautiful island; that tall glass of water standing next to her!'

We laugh loudly. Her eyes grow large like a little child, and she excitably remembers.

'The devil and his wife were fighting that day, you know! It rained but the sun was shining like always. God looking down on His people!' she says.

'Monkey's wedding or not, I think Manley was better looking!' I say.

She smacks my hand mockingly. 'You naughty guurl!' We laugh as I grease her head.

Grandad pretends not to hear anything. Out of nowhere he grabs the remote control and says, 'When a mouse teases a cat, he knows there's a hole nearby, so, carry on Merlene; I hear you, oh! Oluwaseun will leave soon and you will be stuck with me only!'

We all burst out laughing while he feigns a jealous rage.

He puts a local movie on for us, Love and Leprosy.

CHAPTER 19

BUPE KOMBE
LONDON, UK, 2017

I LEAVE THE RUMBLE of Brixton Tube Station, grateful that it's not pissing rain. I haven't been home in about a year. Young mums sport freshly pressed weaves and trendy trainers. Their little ones zoom past me in massive buggies. A few of them have frowning partners at their side. If we used a magic magnifying glass, there would be shoe skid marks on the pavement left behind by the oh-so excited dads.

The streets have changed a lot from when I was little. They have boutiques and cafés, all the things we considered posh back in the day. As I walk along the bright mural walls, I remember being a youngster wanting to create art this beautiful. I pass the house where Mrs Croft lived, and there is a young white couple who live there now with their dog. It's been turned into a studio apartment, and I hear it's quite ritzy on the inside.

Brixton market, thankfully, has some semblance to my once upon a time. Reggae music seeps from the stalls, along with the smell of scotch bonnets, curries and raw meat.

'Cum si wi! Cum si wi!' A dreadlocked man beams in my direction. He has an A-frame board next to him that reads, 'Say no to bombing Syria'.

'Wah yuh ave fi mi?'

'We ave everytin yuh need! Chinese ginja an ginseng… luv potion fi yu lova!'

I shake my head but pump my fist. "One love brethren. Ave a bless day!"

I trot down to the house, hoping that I'm not too late for my chat with Dad. I hold my hand over the door handle for a few seconds. I take a few deep breaths. My racing heart beats from my chest, into my head, and out of my ears. I hang my head low in the hopes to gather strength. I don't want today to end in a fight about my life – to be about the disappointing daughter I have become. I just want to have a nice afternoon with him and share the news about Maggie. I twist the handle and open the door wide. The bell to the ground floor still rings when I walk in, even though the shop has been closed for six years. It makes me think of my nan, and I can't help but miss her. Her last postcard had a picture of her and her friend in their new home at the seaside in Kingston.

'Why, look at you! Come here, sweetheart!'

'Uncle Kabaso!' I kiss my uncle warmly on each cheek and we hug for a full 30 seconds.

'What are you doing here?'

'Well, that's a nice way to say hello to your wee old uncle! Your mum and dad needed some help packing.'

'Geez, go on then. Make me feel bad about not being here.'

'Well, you should, hun. It goes without saying. Which reminds me, how's that ugly mug of a boyfriend you're shacking up with?'

'Leave Jerome alone.'

'On his best day, he makes Shabba Ranks look pretty as a flower.' He clicks his fingers three times in a circle and doubles over. I feign a sulk.

Dad comes downstairs. He's older now. Still lanky, but for the first time, I see speckles of grey lined along his temples. He kisses me on both cheeks and examines me from under his eyelashes as though he has a fringe. My mates used to say he looked at people the way Princess Di did.

I sit down to have a ginger beer. I change my mind and ask for some juice instead, with a slice of toast. Butter and marmite are on my mind. I wish I had stopped at the market to get a lamb curry. But the thought of a massive, juicy mango straight off a tree in Zambia derails me. I picture it bursting in my mouth, its goo coming down my hand. Uncle Kabaso puts some music on, and I remember where I am. I watch them stack some boxes, and they take down the photographs from the hall of fame. The photo of Sam Sharpe is in my father's hands. It disappears into bubble wrap when he begins to talk to me. Pictures of Michelle and Barack are next in line.

'Bupe, your mother has tried to talk to you, but we feel that it's getting us nowhere. Do you remember how well you did when you graduated in Zambia?'

'Dad, I'm still trying to get on my feet. Can't you give me a break?'

'We have, darling. A bloody long one. You've got to talk to us.'

'Why should I? None of you ever talk.'

'What do you want to talk about? Shoot!' He walks towards me.

'OK. Why don't you and Aunty Stella talk to each other like human beings?'

He raises his eyebrows at my question and looks around. His brother nods to him as though to give him consent to finally talk about a secret only they seem to know.

He sits down at the table across from me. His voice is low.

'Bupe, there is a damage that can be left behind by those committed to a struggle. To a fight. I totally get it, Bupe, but you have to learn to live for you. When I was younger, your grandfather was a hero. They shouted his name in the streets. Guards opened gates for him, and his wife rang a bell for house help. But this was after we won independence. Before that, we lived in a two-room house with no electrical connections or running water for that matter. Only a shrub of hibiscus separated us from the neighbours. At times during the week, white inspectors would come to make sure we've cleaned our tiny verandas. They would call your grandfather out to prove that he was capable of cleaning his own floor. Can you imagine how humiliating that was? When it rained, the leaks in our roof were so bad, your grandparents would sometimes stay up at night standing in a corner to watch over us while we slept. Our house was used as an office for freedom fighters, meetings often going on into the middle of the night. The house was always full of people running away, hiding. Ants infested the cracks in the floor in the hot season. Ours was a humble beginning, my dear.

'In a flash, we went from living like that to a large home on the white side of town. The home you've had the privilege of living in with your aunt Stella. Picture it for a second: the wonder of seeing a ring of heat glow on a stove for the first time? And then, before you could say Bob's your uncle, we were whisked off to school here in the Midlands.'

'What's your point, Dad?'

'My point is that the transformation impacted us so much that no one could foresee the family damage it would leave in its wake. No one could see that I'd be sitting here with you, right now, still trying to figure this out. Can't you see?

'Your grandad was liberating the country, while your grandmother felt chained to the life of being his wife. One she didn't know before independence happened. His life was getting better on the outside, and we were suffering on the inside. Aunt Stella derided your grandmother because all the black women she ever saw were her friends' nannies or house help. She began to belittle your grandma, and we spoke to her less and less until we finally lost her.' His eyes water.

Uncle Kabaso comes to put his arm around my shoulder.

'Your dad has tried with your aunt, Bupe. It's not his fault. Hopefully she'll come around soon.'

My father looks at me. 'Bupe, if you need to go back to Zambia, you know you can. Right? We'll support you and make sure you have everything you need.'

I hesitate. I bite my lip. And I look at them. 'I'm a London girl. I always have been. No one is coming on sweeping chariots to take me nowhere. This is where I belong. With Jerome. With you.'

The two men grunt. Uncle Kabaso smacks his forehead and rolls his eyes at me.

'If that boy really loves you, why hasn't he made an honest man of himself? He's too proud to step up and show himself around here?'

'You know how you lot get. I won't let him be insulted by you.'

'Him over us, huh? Well, I'll have you know that you are making your bed, love. So, don't say we didn't warn you.'

I stand to take Marcus Garvey off the wall. I was always drawn to the feather in his hat. I wipe the glass on the frame and wrap him away too.

'I hear Maggie has gone to Lagos. How is that going?'

'I think I may need to go there, Dad. She needs me.'

'Only if you promise to get permission from Abisola. This is about your cousin, not about you. Should you decide to, you've got to promise to stay in a decent hotel somewhere safe. I don't want anything happening to you there. And it's better to have somewhere for your cousin to go if things don't go according to plan. We've got quite a bit in from the sale of this house. We can afford a bit of a splash. I'll call him in a bit. I found him and got his number when I heard Maggie was going.'

'Thanks, Dad. But let's see. Maybe I won't have to go after all. I'll keep in touch with Maggie in the meantime.'

'That's fine. But I have one last condition. If you do go, once you get back here, you get yourself a job and stick with it! Then, we can begin our plans to go visit your grandad in Chinsali in a couple of months. He's not been too well, I'm afraid. The doctors say we only have the rest of this year with him.'

I turn my back to them. A tear falls, camouflaged by the

translucent pellets of bubble wrap. I seal it with another face from history, and I picture my grandfather's being put away, packed into the box marked 'to go.'

CHAPTER 20

GRANDMOTHER MARGARET
LUSAKA, ZAMBIA, 1964

'ARE YOU READY TO go, Bana CJ?'

Charles's voice shook the house as Margaret folded and pressed down her ear to pick out her afro evenly. She looked in the mirror at the chitenge dress which bore Kaunda's face on it in four places. She wondered if she should have designed something more modern, like Mrs Kaunda's champagne-coloured robe, which was done by the Ginsberg lady. It flowed like butter, with embroidery stitch detail across the chest and at the knee. Or perhaps a something more dramatic like Jackie Onassis or Mrs Coretta King. Charles had insisted she get something from London, but she had been determined to wear this dress, so it was too late to turn back now. 'Zambia, Zambia,' she whispered to herself. She smiled. At last, they had come to the end of the journey. Hopefully the beginning of a new one for her family.

The two room house was a flurry of excitement, all their personal effects packed and ready to be taken to the new home. Neighbours filled their veranda and garden, waiting to escort them into their car. The boys wore their Sunday best, and Charles was beaming profusely. Stella had left early in the morning as she would be performing callisthenics at the stadium. Outside, her husband bent to pluck a flower from the hedge next to the car. He placed a red hibiscus in her hair, and he kissed her on the cheek. She blushed and all the spectators clapped for them.

'I wonder what the Princess Royal will be wearing?' she said.

'No, my love, don't bother yourself with that. You look so beautiful. You were right to insist on traditional for a once in a lifetime night like this. It shows your commitment to the struggle, to the party – which we should never forget. You look like the wife of a freedom fighter. A minister perhaps?' They laughed together.

CJ asked, 'Is it true that Prime Minister Kaunda will be arriving in the Kwacha car?'

'What do you know about the Kwacha car?'

'Kwacha car is amazing, Tata!' said CJ.

Margaret looked at her son, who was now stretching into a tall young man. At this rate, he would be as big as his father, but perhaps not so heavy set.

'Dad, the car is made of copper! Can you believe it? It's got white leather seats, and it's a left-hand drive. It's all electric controlled with power steering! Is it true it cost £38,000?'

'No son, it's not made of copper – technically – it's moss gold. And it cost about a tenth of that – £3,800.' He laughed at the boy heartily.

'It's still a lot to be spending on one individual, for one day,' Margaret whispered under her breath.

'What did you say?' he turned his full weight towards her.

'Nothing, Bashi CJ. Nothing. We are ready to go now.'

She smiled widely. He looked at her for a moment. She turned to usher the boys into their seats, and she heard him suck his teeth behind her.

They climbed into their car, which was chauffeur driven. Margaret continued to smile, and her husband held her hand. 'Let's not fight tonight. It's special for all of us.'

'I'm sorry, Bashi CJ. I'll be more careful with my words.'

The children from all the other houses swarmed the car to wave and clap them away until they were small enough to vanish from the side mirrors.

*

The stadium teemed with people from all walks of life. Almost 200,000 people filled the seats while marching trumpets and drums exploded in the air. Margaret had never seen so many people in one place. Multicoloured balloons floated everywhere with the president-designate's face on them. Children marched, waving life size flags from around the world.

During a short recess, her husband attended to some delegates, and so Margaret took leave to use the powder room.

'Dearest Margaret, is that you?' The familiar husky voice came from behind her, taking her by surprise. 'Come and join us at the back. I'm due to perform in an hour.'

'Fabiola, how are you?'

'I am tres jolie, ma soeur. It's a great day for you and Charles, non?'

'Thank you. Yes, it is. I didn't know that you were back from Congo.'

'Charles and the organising committee begged me to come. They remember all the sacrifice we made too you know!'

Margaret nodded her head too fast.

'It is a surprise for everyone. Top secret, even for the audience – so of course, they did not put it in the program.'

'Well, yes, let me come with you and see the action at the back. I need to check on my daughter, Stella. She's been training for many months now with the Israeli instructors. They did a wonderful job at Malawi Independence too.'

'Ah, very good, but I do not think that you will find her backstage. There are too many people. Come with me.'

In the private booth, she watched Fabiola gurgle her gin and rub her throat while a team of people did her makeup. Unexpected sounds escaped her throat as she prepared to sing on stage.

'How rude of me. Would you like some of this?' She passed her a glass of gin.

Margaret hesitated. Before she could answer, symbols clanged outside and drums continued to beat. The gown was wheeled in, hoisted up on rails.

Sapphire blue, sparkling all through. Her heart fell to her feet. She caught a glimpse of herself in the full length swing mirror, wrapped in chitenge pictures of the new president. Her leg of mutton sleeves suddenly felt old fashioned and unflattering.

Fabiola climbed into the dress, nimble as an antelope. Local emeralds were clasped around her neck and small stones hung at her ears.

'You look like a dream.'

'Thank you, Margaret. I am glad you like it. I will have it sent specially to you as a souvenir for today, and also for you to remember what we went through together.' She bent down and kissed her fully on the lips.

'You better go back out so you can clap for me, eh? I don't know if the others will, but with you, at least I know I got a friend.'

The scent of gin and cigarettes lingered on Margaret's lips. She wanted to take a handkerchief to wipe it away, but instead, her fingers swiped gently across her lips. It felt good. She hurried to join Charles while masked traditional dancers concluded their performance. The lights dimmed, and voices hushed.

Out of nowhere, Fabiola's voice pierced through the stadium. She sang a sweet melody which moved them to tears. When the tempo changed, Charles's face did too. All the men watched her in a trance. Margaret squeezed his hand. He did not squeeze back.

Finally, the time they had all been waiting for came. The last line of 'God Save the Queen' ended in a drum roll and the stadium plunged into darkness. The Union Jack and the Governor's Standard was lowered. Fanfare sounded over the hushed stadium. A beam of light cut through the night air and a spotlight trained on the Zambian flag. It was hoisted from the foot of the flagstaff ever so slowly. It burst bright in green, orange, red, and black. At the stroke of midnight, the Zambian anthem begun. It was 'Nkosi Sikelel' iAfrika', but the words were new. In English.

The air force thundered through the sky. Cheers and lights. Fireworks whistled into the air and burst into falling raindrops. For the first time in her life, under a bright lit sky, Margaret saw her husband cry.

A flame was lit that night. It burned bright and hopeful for their new country.

*

Later, after she put the children to bed in their self-contained rooms on the other side of the house, she took a walk in her brand new home. She switched the lights on and off, just because she could and partly because she was bored. Out of habit, she lit a paraffin lamp – in spite of Charles' instruction, she still preferred to call it koloboi. She let its flickers guide her downstairs. It's scent and warmth brought her comfort. At the minibar, she opened a bottle of Mellow Wood brandy. She switched on their new radiogram to dance alone. She twisted to the 'Mashed Potato'. The dance felt strange to her, it made her laugh out loud. She imagined an audience clapping for her, and one person stepping forward just to say thank you. She waited all night in the paraffin lit room, but Charles did not come.

It would be the first time that Margaret's world turned black.

CHAPTER 21

MAGGIE OLUWASEUN AYOMIDE
LAGOS, NIGERIA, 2017

LAGOS HAS NO SPACE for nothingness. Something fills up everything. Everyone makes something from nothing. In Lusaka, what would be manicured grass bordered by rose bushes will have some kind of built structure – with a full family in it. Other times a shop, or tailor's room, or restaurant, and possibly something else on top of that. They build houses with three sides, the fourth along the boundary wall. It makes me wonder what would happen if there had to be a hole blown into the shared wall – would one neighbour end up in the other's home? Can one put windows in? The thought of windows on a shared wall makes me laugh.

We drive to Akute to see 'the time capsule', as my father says. It is another house that his family has had since he was a teenager. The flat where my grandparents currently stay is for the convenience of nursing and amenities, 'closer to everything,' he says.

The Pentecostal nature of Nigerians is evident in the names of churches, schools, and hospitals: Seeds of Covenant School, Peculiar People's Church. The roads take us through dips and potholes, through swampy areas thick with palm forests.

Trees line the way as we pass between the nine hills of Ibadan, heading towards Ogun State. Industry does not sleep. Couches on display – tan, grey, leatherine, polyester florals – along with tables, clothes – everyone sells something.

We finally get to the house – 'our home', he says. I haven't been here since I was three. It pulls me to it with flashes of memory: running down the stairs, fleeing tickles from my grandfather. I see my mother dressed in the same fabric as my father, and they show me off at parties, so I am handed from relative to relative.

The monstrosity of a house greets us. A flat roofed, double storey house with large entertainment space on marble verandas. It stands tall, full of untold stories from a lifetime ago. Green creepers along the mushroom-coloured walls reveal a once kempt garden. An acre of grass and tropical fruit trees dot the land to the left of it. Muscular redhead lizards dash about with dense-sounding footsteps, and I hold onto my father's shoulder. His arm protectively swoops me out of the way when one drops from the pipe. It lifts its head, showing off its wellbuilt chest.

'That is so weird, Dad! What is it doing?' I'm still holding on to him, looking at the lizard from behind him.

'There is a common saying here, that when the redhead falls down but lands safely, he does that to tell you that he has not hurt himself. In other words, if no one will praise you, don't forget to do it yourself!' He chuckles.

I titter in response, wondering if he's always had such self-regard, or it really is just a proverb. He turns to face me, smiling, and I take a moment to watch the small details about him. It's like he's a star in a favourite movie, and I finally have this shot to watch him all by myself. No audience. No mum, no grandparents, no one. I am in a cinema for one. His face is clean shaven again, exposing the dimple in his chin. I want to reach out and put my pinkie in it, but instead I put my hands back into the pockets of my jeans. His eyes have brackets of little trenches around them, and they get rounder when he smiles.

I turn my stare to the boastful reptile, not because of Dad's joke, but because in Zambia, we have bluehead lizards. From what I see, they are the opposite to redheads. Blueheads, gumu-gumu, walk in slow motion and hesitate before they take their next step, silent in their gait. They are shy, and as children, we would find them smashed flat, like cardboard cuttings pasted with glue along the street. If they fell out of a eucalyptus tree, I am certain that they would splatter everywhere. The kids used to say that is how they bore their young – with a suicidal long-drop. Perhaps if I were a lizard, I would be a combination of the two. A mutated African lizard. Purplehead. Fast, fierce, and showy with my work.

Slow and unsure with matters of the heart.

We walk to the grand entrance of the house.

The heavy front door creaks as we open it. The subtle feeling of silk cobwebs and invisible dust mites greets my skin, giving me goose bumps on a hot afternoon. The paralysing smell of musty carpets and mothballs salutes our nostrils. The Jamaican coat of arms is the first thing I see on the wall. 'Out of Many, One People' is written on a ribbon at the bottom. Two people, an Indian looking man and woman, stand upright on either side of an English looking shield that is lined with pineapples along its red cross. A crocodile sits at the top of the badge.

An old telephone sits on a wooden table with a phone directory from the early 1990s. The living room is empty of furniture, but the dining table is an ode to Jamaica: mats, maps, and whisky glasses all replete with the black, green, and yellow flag. The shelves are adorned with framed photos and curios from different countries.

Grandfather's office is a room dedicated to his achieve-ments. Photographs with presidents, governors, and billionaires.

The room animates my father. He narrates the story of how his father created a magnificent business from humble beginnings; how savvy he was, and how his work took him around the world. I find a stack of business cards that read, 'Ayomide & Son'.

'Wow, Dad! Are these from the firm you and Grandpa had? What a memento!'

He quickly takes the cards from me and walks out to the hallway. 'Well, yes, we had a firm together. But it didn't last long. I wanted to be my own man, you know?'

'Yes, I know actually.'

'She told you?'

'Yes, she did. But none of that matters to me. I know that you wanted the best for us, but things didn't work out. Right?'

He looks at me carefully, as though searching my face. Maybe to catch a hint of sarcasm, but he doesn't find it because I believe in my heart, that he wouldn't have done anything to hurt us on purpose. He seems reassured by the steadiness of my gaze.

'I've forgiven you, Dad. Honestly. Have they?' I point at his parents' wedding photo.

'I think I've made my amends.'

'I have a country marketing firm you know,' I say.

He turns his focus to me, an eyebrow raised with interest.

'Investment promotions,' I offer, wondering if he wants to know more about my business.

He bobs his head in encouragement.

'When I stand in front of investors from all over the world, I watch my words take their breath away. I awe them with the enchantment of our resources, our people. I sell them a dream. A dream of fortunes and treasures. Of impact and development.' I sweep the room with my hands melodramatically as though there is a large audience before us. I touch his arm warmly.

'Perhaps I get this from your side of the family.'

He claps his hands, and he looks impressed. He begins

with his Naija accent, 'See diz bright apple has fallen close to di tree, oh.' He laughs, retreating into his English inflection.

'You see, that's how I used to feel when I was younger,' he continues. 'Your grandad had been in commodities trading since I was a little boy. His business mushroomed into a decent fortune, but by the time you came, he still hadn't adapted his wind sails to the new direction the world was taking. For example,' he pushed his glasses back up his moist nose.

'Do you know when the first ATM was ever installed?'

'No.'

'In 1967, in North London. Enfield. Barclays did it. And your grandad? Said he could never trust a machine with his cash. And to be fair, he never ever has.'

We cackle in unison.

'After years and years of watching New York perform so well, bringing in the top guys to make presentations to him, I thought it was time. I was so frustrated because we kept missing such a wonderful opportunity to invest and grow our capital base. Year in, year out, I begged him. You see, I had bigger dreams. I wanted us to diversify. To invest back into Africa. To build roads and banks, to create worlds that gave us a long-lasting inheritance here! On our soil!' It was his turn to perform in front of his imaginary audience, an audience that included his father.

'So, you did, right?' I ask.

'Yes, I did. But unfortunately, my timing was an ineffaceable blunder. I lost much more than I ever could have imagined.' He takes the stack of cards out of my hand and places them back on the wooden desk. He holds my own hands.

'Ayomide & Son.' He gazes at the deck of cards.

'You never know in this life. Imagine it; hold it for a second.' His eyes twinkle, and he whispers, 'Ayomide and Daughter.'

I let the magic fill my belly. There are tingles in my hands as his hold mine. I smile broadly, and it feels as though I'm in the middle of a dream.

'Come this way! We came so I could show you our house. Your home.'

As I walk behind him, I try to block out the images of the newspaper cuttings I found in my mother's room the day she cut her hair. The headings jump out all around the room, but they are taken away by a steady, far reaching arm. It is a settling feeling, and I am sure that it is God. It is His will for me to be reunited with my father. God will look after me as he always has. This time I've been made to understand what happened. He means well, my Dad. I'm just like him, right? He can't have known that Black Monday would hit when it did. He only wants the best for us. For me.

We climb the staircase, flanked by a terraced wall of photographs of my father as a baby, and gradually to his days at boarding school, and later, university. The pictures that hang in the corridor to the bedrooms show his other children and his wife, and it makes me wince in spite of myself. To the left of the hall, he shows me his room and demonstrates with a childlike elation how he used to sneak out from his balcony as a teenager.

In the pictures, his wife is blonde, and her eyes are a light brown, like the back of a camel. Her skin looks like it's had its fair share of cooking in tanning beds, but then again, it might be a natural result of leisure time spent on the decks of yachts I see along the wall. I wonder if her hair is bleached. Her smiles reveal a line of expensive dentures, probably done in some place like Turkey. Her breasts burst out to the sides like bowling balls, round and unnaturally high – chesticles. Yes, I think that that would be the most suitable description for her inflatable front. Her muddy mascara is reminiscent of the beautiful elephants I had lunch with in Livingstone a few weeks ago. Too much. Dirty but pretty. Someone should tell Chesticle Charleen that less can be more. Her suits look like the kind you buy in Harrods or, in their case, Lafayette Paris. Her nails are perfect gels set in scarlet and her jewellery looks burdensome.

Her children, 'the boys', she has two. One 23, the other 21.

They are short but handsome, skin brown as her eyes, flanking her in most of the photographs. They are here, captured in all their outdoor pursuits. Cricket, swimming, horse riding, and taekwondo. Why are the emotions in my belly so childlike? So unreasonable? I feel a tug at my heart. It makes me want to explode and smother this wall with its perfectly framed lives with all of my insides. Instead I smile, and the sides of my face ache with the strain.

Finally, we go upstairs to his parents' room and, as if to soothe me, he tells me exactly where to go; the side of the bed where my grandmother used to sleep. There is a framed photograph of me as a baby at my christening. My ears are studded with almond shaped earrings, just visible through a soft afro, and I am dressed in a pure white dress. In the picture, I am being kissed by both parents while my grandmother looks on happily, a dimple in her cheek. He shows me her diaries, and in them she has marked my birthday and written a prayer for my wellbeing religiously, every year since the divorce. They all start with something like this:

'Dear Heavenly Father,
It's Maggie's birthday today. I wonder what she is doing this very moment. I hope that she remembers us, may she have the strength and guidance of Your Holy Spirit, and may she inherit the strong character of her people before her. May she live in peace and may she never feel she is alone.'

I shiver. My grandparents had not forgotten me. Having to unlearn in a moment what has lived in my heart over the decades – both intentionally and unintentionally – by my mother's words, by my beliefs. I pass my fingers over her words for each year, and I close my eyes to picture her pain – and to remember mine. The smell of the musty paper, the smoothness of the ink, I try to keep in my memory. To lock it up where there once was emptiness. How do you take all of this feeling and preserve it in a bottle – forever? What would its price be?

'I have another surprise for you, angel.'

Did he call me 'angel'? Oh Lord, You are gracious. I look up at him, trying to squeeze my tears back to where they came from. He rummages through a drawer and pulls out Eleanor. The soft doll I lost the night we left London for good. 'The airport called home and said you had left it. I kept her for the day you would return.' I hug him like I'm a little girl again, and I take a deep breath of his scent. It's not desperation anymore. It is simply love; pure love.

Afterwards, he shows Eleanor and I photographs from his secondary school days with Uncle CJ. The two of them standing out like sore thumbs – handsome ones though. Uncle CJ, tall and in the back row. Dad, shorter and seated in the front. Lines of boys in striped rugby jerseys, dorm masters, and friends in common rooms.

'Well, at least you and Uncle CJ actually made the photos black and white.'

We laugh at this.

'I was so lucky to have him as a friend, you know. It was difficult those days. I mean, don't get me wrong, we were quite the popular lads, and we were both excellent at sports, academics – we nailed it every time. But there was something missing when one wanted to talk about "home". How do you explain the salty crunch and the bursting goo of dodo to someone who doesn't know it?' He laughs.

'And. CJ always, he was always there for me' He lowers his eyes but does not finish his sentence. Looking at the photograph intensely, he takes a deep breath. 'Never mind. Let's move on to the last room. I know you'll love it!'

He takes me to the next room and opens the door slowly – it is so magical; I jump up and down with the glee of a four year old. Books line the walls from floor to ceiling. A mobile ladder tempting me to my favourite indulgence, beckoning me to the heights of the shelves. The scent of old leather. Some classic collections are locked up in glass cases. I gasp in awe, thumbing through the spines of books lined in rows of labelled shelving. I pick some up, blowing away the dust from their covers. I am teleported to the gateways of multiple universes, but I have to remind myself that I cannot read them all at once.

Most of the local books have one thing in common. They all have the spidery scribbles from authors thanking my grandparents or wishing them well.

'Did Grandma and Grandpa attend that many book signings?'

'Everyone in Lagos is an author, baby. Our neighbours' neighbours, family friends, strangers. They have all written something. If it is not about themselves, it is about their spouse.' My father laughs. 'We are natural storytellers.'

I stand back, impressed and moved at the same time. I ask for one thing out of this entire room of precious leather-bound knowledge – my grandmother's handwritten book of Jamaican recipes.

CHAPTER 22

BUPE KOMBE
LONDON, UK, 2017

TODAY'S BEEN A SHIT day. My back burned from fatigue after I sat up all night waiting for Jerome to come home – he didn't. When I eventually got the chance to close my eyes, a baby wailed through the thin walls of our flat. My nose twitched and my belly somersaulted from a stench so rank, it smelt like our new neighbour was cooking something that died last year. Later, I went to another interview, this time at an art gallery in Clapham. I could barely keep my eyes open through the geezer's questions. I passed through Tesco on my way back home. I used some dosh I scooped off Dad and managed to get enough groceries to last Jerome and me the week. In between the aisles, I picked up a bag of purple grapes and scoffed them down while I did my shopping. The lady at the counter, her chair as high as a tennis umpire, balked at me, pointing at the drool on my bottom lip. I wiped my mouth with the back of my sleeve and gave her the empty packet. All it had left was a bar code. In all fairness, the bag wasn't completely empty. It still had a few pips and miniature branches.

The chemist down the road compelled me to enter it. Just to check, right? My mind replayed all the food I've been eating lately, the sleepiness, and the mood swings. It started to rain soon as I came out the store, and now I'm soaked to the bone as I get home.

Labouring up the stairs, drum and bass blares from different speakers. A teenage couple block my way as they sit in the stairway, enveloped in each other, groping one other under their coats. 'Get a room!' I yell at them. They carry on as though the survival of the world is reliant upon their procreation.

In the frame of a window, a Pakistani housewife is having it out with her husband. He runs out of the flat, and a flying mug follows him, missing his head only by an inch. I finally get to our floor. I open the door; the chain is still on. I bang on it, and Jerome takes his sweet time. A whirlwind seems to have come through our flat and left all our personal effects in its wake. Plates of food and empty bottles of beer are strewn all over the floor. I walk in, and he barely looks away from his video game.

'Could you fix me a cuppa, babe? I'm freezing.' My teeth are chattering. I get no response. I'm greeted by the back of his head as I carry in all the bags, one by one, dripping from the rain outside.

'Someone's been shopping, I see.'

'How can you see if your eyes are glued to your telly, Jerome? Could you help me bring them in please?'

'If I stop now, I'm going to lose. I'll do it in a sec,' he says, never once looking at me.

'But it can't wait a sec. I've come up all the way by myself, and if we leave these in the hallway, you know they'll get nicked in a heartbeat.'

He doesn't answer me. He twists his tongue while he presses his control pad.

He shouts with victory and yells at the top of his voice. A thud-thud comes from upstairs, 'Shut it, you wanker!'

'Go suck your mum!'

'Jerome! Come on. We have to live with these people.' I

drag in the last bag and make a dash for the bathroom. I'm bursting, and I need to see what that stick says. I sit on the toilet and pee onto it with both relief and fear.

'Oi, wots the matter with you?'

'I'm peeing on a stick, Jerome. I think we might be – you know!'

Thud thud on the roof again, this time above the bathroom.

I look at the two blue lines on the pregnancy strip for the tenth time. How could I be pregnant? I look at my reflection in the mirror. My green eyes, almost hazel, changing with emotion.

'Yo! Wagwan? Are we safe, babe?' he shouts from the other room.

'Safe?' I snigger.

'Well, wa u saying?' It tires him, waiting.

I open the door carefully. 'We're – preggers, Jerome,' I say. He gives me a smile and turns back to his game. 'Pucker up, sweet pea. You know my bad boys swim like there ain't no tomorrow! Just stay peng for me.'

'Peng? Is that all you're going to say? You're only worried about how I'll look?' No response.

My hands quiver as I reach the rail for my towel, but it's soaking wet and heaped on the floor. 'That's it!' I scream, bursting out of the bathroom.

'Jerome, I've done everything in my power to live up to our promise. "Together forever" you once told me. "Through thick and thin, no matter what." But what have you done for me? Tell me! What have you sacrificed for me? What? Will you help me look after a baby if we have one?'

'What are you on about? I'm with you, ain't I? I'm right here. I stayed with you like I said I would, so what more do you want?'

'I want a family, Jerome.'

'I'm your family.'

I look at the couch he lies on. An oil stain on the coarse fabric makes me cringe. Dried up goat curry has caked on a bowl, bright orange, and it sits right next to his trainers. Its cracks trace through the hardened oil, and I recoil from deep down inside.

'Let's go to Africa. Meet my people. Come give it a try. See where I'm from! Maybe we can start a new life there. Maybe you can have a business there. Something legit, Jerome. We can't raise a baby like this.' My arms are flailing in the air. He is quiet for a long while, and he looks at me intently.

'Me? Africa? You serious? What kind of dumb shit is that?'

The feeling of phantom limb from amputation. Cut off from my land, my people, my roots. People, who for me are still there, but I've made pretend aren't. All for what? For this?

In our room, I look for my green and blue chitenge with the guinea fowl prints. It sits folded crisply. It's as new as the day Aunt Stella gave it to me. I spread it out on the bed and put all my clothes on it. Some books, a few pairs of jeans, my favourite sweater. I tie it into a bundle and strap it onto my back like a baby in Chinsali, over one shoulder and under my arm. I walk towards the door.

'Goodbye, Jerome.'

'You'll be back, sweet pea. And I'll be right here waiting for you.'

'Two billion, Jerome!'

'You wot?'

'Two billion people in this world are Commonwealth citizens. That means we are all the product of colonialisation, of migration, slave trade, one thing or the other; we all found ourselves here because the Crown took a look at the beautiful places we come from and said, "Hey, guess what? We want in!" A lot of fucked up shit went down, but what matters is the plenty of beautiful things that came out of it too. If it hadn't happened, I wouldn't be here today. I wouldn't have known you. I wouldn't have had more than one country to call my own. I am half African and half Jamaican, Jerome, and that will never ever change. Your child will be African too. The sooner you accept that, the better for you. We are all equal!'

'You having a laugh?'

'Not this time, I'm afraid. It's a shame, Jerome, that you can't see what you are blessed with because the world needs you. The kids here need you. When are you going to stand up and be counted?'

I walk out and leave the door wide open behind me. Let him get up and close it for a change.

CHAPTER 23

MAGGIE OLUWASEUN AYOMIDE
LAGOS, NIGERIA, 2017

On the fifth day, my father invites me for a drink on the island. We cross the Lagos Bridge at great speed, veering around potholes and strewn rubbish. At this rate, I am certain that a human corpse would not be good enough reason to slow down. My braids are flying all over the place, and my scarlet stained lips are dry from the wind. By the time I get there, I will look like I have been blowing hot coals to make a fire for supper.

This is not at all how I fantasised my first drive across the monumental bridge would be. It was supposed to be slow, a fabulous procession, like the music videos on Trace: me dressed up in Versace, and Tiwa Savage giving me a high five while we go for a night out on the town in an impressive, shiny, all black convoy with Tekno and Starboy. Instead, I hold my chest with one hand and the handle of the roof with the other, as though ready for anything.

'Please slow down, Dad! I'm freaking out!'

'We can't afford to drive slowly. They could hijack us – this is Lagos oh! I keep telling you, angel, these people have all kinds of tricks!' I am a cat on a hot tin roof about this new possibility. Kidnap or a tyre burst flipping us into the Lagos River – I am not sure which headline would be worse.

Then, finally, some calm.

The city morphs into a land of modern highways and lights, with tarred roads and outdoor advertising screens at well kept roundabouts. A far cry from the mainland. I remember Bola in his 100% Dolce & Gabbana shirt and understand now why he was disappointed. I throw my head back and laugh.

Ikoyi Hotel towers above the highway. White. Immaculate. Porters in tailored jackets take deep bows to welcome us. The classical music in the lobby sets the stage as the lights dance against the polished marble and chrome. It smells of soap and luxury. We go out to the open-air clubhouse on the first floor.

The evening is cool, and the aircon provides relief from the activities of the day. The river boasts an exclusive boat club next to the hotel and a breath-taking skyline of prime Lagos real estate.

My father examines the menu while he takes a sip of his red and black Gulden.

The waiter pours my green and blue Star.

Dad takes off his spectacles to wipe them clean.

'How is your mother?'

'Fine. Busy. Rescuing the world as always,' I say.

'And your husband?' He looks at me, holding my eyes with his, only for a moment.

I look away, wondering why I am never able to mask my emotions. 'He's OK.'

'OK?'

'Yes, Dad. OK.'

'You know, my darling, whatever is bothering you, I hope you will figure it out soon. I've not seen you running to answer your phone or pining for him. You've not mentioned him once since you got here.' His eyes search mine for some emotion, but I am prepared this time – I don't give him the satisfaction.

'Try to spend time with your grandparents, and I promise you, it may change your perspective on whatever you are going through.'

I gulp my Star and bite into a yam chip.

The Lagos River dances, showing off its billionaire boats. I finally take the time to appreciate its elegant beauty. A toothless man walks in with Uncle Tayo, catching us in this moment.

'Abisola, my man! You did not tell me dat you have taken anoda wife now?' the old man says teasingly with his mouth wide open, so much that you can see to the watermelon-pink of his throat. He breathes through his mouth as his nose sounds blocked. His tongue retracts like a snake about to strike, while he waits for the effect of his joke. 'Please, abeg, tell me where you found this beauty, me sef I am getting tired of my own wife, ooh! She has become shrewish with old age!'

We all laugh, and thankfully, I am introduced as Abs's long-lost Zambian daughter.

'Ehen, while you are here, do not tell them dat your father is half Yoruba and especially half Edo. They will respect you more if you sound exotic – Zambian sounds better.'

They sit close to us but out of earshot to discuss business issues.

'How is your uncle CJ? I knew him first, you know. A superb man.'

'Yes, Dad, you and Mum both told me.'

He looks out to the skyline. His eyes are those of a man with plenty to say, but not sure how.

'And where is Charleen – my stepmother?' I ask, trying to take control of the conversation. 'I thought she would be here.'

'Things are a little complicated, my angel. She's been focusing on her new job in Paris. She couldn't get time off as you can imagine.'

'I see,' I say.

'Is she not here because I am?'

He gulps his beer again and takes back the wheel. 'Do your mother and uncle talk to each other now?'

'Sort of. The relationship is still strained, Dad.'

He lights a cigarette and asks me with raised eyebrows if I mind. I shrug, and he drags on his cigarette, tapping its long end into a heavy glass ashtray. I have another chip. He exhales the smoke as well as the story trapped inside him.

'Your mother never forgave him for not telling her about the death of their mother. Your grandfather was a hard man, and he gave clear instructions to your uncle not to tell his siblings. In fact, he got the news when he was at our house in London. In those days we would never dream of defying our parents.'

'So, how did she find out; I mean what happened to Grandma in the first place? Why would anyone not tell their child that their mother drowned and died, if she did?'

He shakes his head slowly while looking out to the river. 'Baby, I'm sorry to break it to you like this, but it wasn't as simple as that. Your grandmother was a serious alcoholic. The domestic staff found her floating in the swimming pool when your mother was only 15. I feel you are old enough now to know what happened.'

I am feeling slightly dizzy, and the aircon is too high. My stomach is turning and suddenly my yam chips are bland and chunky.

'Dad, I—'

'If your mother gets mad at me for telling you, that is her own wahala, but you deserve to know the truth.'

The breeziness in his voice infuriates me. My cheeks become heated with rage, my heart beats uncontrollably, my throat is suddenly parched. It makes my voice hoarse and low. Words tumble out of my mouth without pause.

'The truth? What is the truth, Daddy? That the last time I saw you, you nearly killed my mother in front of me? That you left us in Zambia and you never turned back? That your new marriage and shiny new children replaced me, and I was shelved like an old piece of furniture? Just forgotten! All for what? Some new woman?'

He takes off his glasses to wipe his eyes.

'My truth, Daddy, is waiting by the telephone for you to call because you said you were coming to get me. Suitcase packed and all. Goodbyes said – dressed for my flight with my ticket and passport staring back at me from my bed. You, a world away on the phone, at check-in time asking why I am not on the plane. Me, crying myself to sleep with Ba Mailesi, who may be the only person in this whole world who truly felt my pain. My truth is that I'm seeing you now.' My voice tapers off into a whimper. 'When I'm in my thirties, Dad. Where have you been?'

'Baby, it – it didn't happen like that. I was broken too, so devastated when I had to leave you and when the court ruled in your mother's favour. I can never, ever go back, but I would like for us to try to move forward. What you have done by coming here, my daughter, I pray will begin the process of forgiveness. There are many things I did – I was young and foolish – but my intention was always good. It is true, I put you and your mother in harm's way, I made a major financial move without consulting her. In hindsight, she was right. But at the time, I thought I was invincible. Failure was nothing I had ever truly known. Until you.'

I blow my nose with a serviette. I pull out my phone to check my face.

He laughs at me. 'Don't worry, even with panda eyes, you are still beautiful.' His attempt to break the ice falls flat.

'Your mother, she was a tough one. She was so heartbroken from the demise of your grandmother – whom she had never been nice to.'

'What do you mean she had never been nice to her?' I ask, revolted again, like this man is now clutching at straws, desperate to make his ex-wife, his ex-family, look bad.

'As a child, your mother thought she was oyinbo do you know what that means? She thought she was white, and your grandmother was a simple village woman and that ate her up.'

'I'm confused, Daddy. Ate who up?'

'Stella had a complex about being black and African. Your grandfather sent her to the best of English boarding schools from a tender age. I think, in her own way, all she wanted to do was fit into this foreign place they had sent her. Her own mother embarrassed her.'

'But that doesn't sound like Mum. You're making things up so you can blame her for something. I mean she is a member of parliament, back home. She stands at rallies, campaigns in the remotest of villages, speaks four local languages impeccably, and you want to tell me Mum thought she was white?'

He laughs mysteriously. 'There is a saying your grandfather likes: "Oria non bie omon asuke, ole len borhe khuale ye!" The mother of a baby with a hunchback knows how she carries the child.'

I stiffen, and fling my braids over my shoulders.

'Life has a funny way of changing our perceptions and growing us up, baby. And that happened to her. When your grandfather first fell out with the ruling party in Zambia, he took a hard stance against a very serious anti-Western campaign that was done through the youth wing – and they were ruthless. Those kids would harass girls in miniskirts; threatening to unhem them with scissors. Women with perms were at risk of getting their hair cut short if they so much as stepped into town. A group of them cut your grandfather's tie in protest of Westernised dress, and after that, they beat him to a pulp. It was all over the papers. Total disrespect, and his old friends did nothing. They were too scared.

'Two things happened to your mother that took her to the other extreme. First, she spent more time with her aunts from Chinsali and made it a life journey to understand the values of her late mother. Second, when your grandfather was "arrested"' – he used his fingers to make quotations in the air – 'she quickly learned that if she were to survive in Zambian society – actually not just survive, but have a genuine impact, enough to vindicate him – then she would have to learn the Zambian way and its politics. She's done well, I can't lie.'

'No one has ever told me what really happened to him. He never talks about it. Where was he taken and why?'

'They banished your grandfather after he was caught

"allegedly" conspiring with some other gentlemen to start a coup. There was a police raid on his house in the middle of the night. He and his closest friends were accused of causing an inferno, one that killed a half a dozen people on the Copperbelt. It saw the end of his career. Their lives transformed dramatically. No one would talk to them. Everyone they had once known, everyone they had grown up with, treated your family like it had the plague. But—' He paused.

'The crux of the matter remains that your mother wanted to make it up to your grandmother. To be more Bemba than the Bemba – because your grandmother was the epitome of traditional elegance. She was the glue, the centre of the family, and once she was gone, it all fell apart. Stella was too young to see this while she was still alive.'

I take in a deep breath. So surprised that mother has revealed none of this to me. Militant and self-sufficient as always. A survivor.

'Do you miss Mum?' I strain to keep my voice steady, to hide how much his answer means to me.

'Your mother and I, angel, we were good friends. Do I wish it worked out? Yes. Do I miss her? No.' He winks, and we chuckle between my sniffles. 'Come now, let's have some Lagos fun. These rendezvous only happen every couple of decades – don't you think?'

His phone flashes, and I see Chesticle Charleen's picture spilling out of the screen. He excuses himself to take her call. He goes quite a distance to take it.

I marvel as everyone effortlessly mouths the words to Davido's 'If'. The 'gb' sounds in Yoruba, they don't just rest at my ears, they vibrate through my bones. They occupy every part of my body. In Bemba, our 'b's are soft like Bupe's name – like it starts with a soft V. The pidgin in the song makes me laugh – it is so liberating to be able to speak simplified English – I wish I could sing along like everyone else.

It's the way I always feel in Zambia – not being able to speak Bemba is so limiting. Always just able to get by, but never enough to feel something from the inside out and bring it to life with ancient African dialect. Having to water down emotions with English vowels is most frustrating. The festive atmosphere sweeps me along with it and I join in.

'Tarty billion for di accounti oh!' I shout with glee – this will have to do for now.

When I'm getting into the swing of things, a voice breaks across the room, and I freeze in a stunned shock. I cannot believe it. I hear my cousin shout, 'Rice and peas or jolloff tonight?'

I scan the room.

'Ah! Rum and coke or a Guinness Malt?'

We scream together, jumping like little girls. Mouths open, shrieks escaping them. I can't believe she came. She's right here.

I look at my dad, and he smiles a big smile. 'Surprise, angel!' I can't believe he's done this for me.

I guess we're going to be alright.

CHAPTER 24

BUPE KOMBE
LAGOS, NIGERIA, 2017

I BELIEVE IT WAS Jane Austen in one of her works who noted how many more handsome men there were in Bath than there were in London. I could say the exact same thing about Lagos. The men here are incredibly statuesque. Uncle Abs and Uncle Tayo gave us a lift to a club in Lekki, and they dished us a wad of Naira. Maggie's in a sulk because she wanted to eat somewhere sane. I say we only have a couple of days here, so we might as well enjoy it. 'What's your poison?' I ask.

'Soda water and lime please.'

'No way cuz, unless you're having a dash of vodka with that.'

She shakes her head but smiles back at me.

Maggie looks beautiful, kissed by the soft lighting of reds and oranges against her dark skin. She really has evolved from the awkward grim statue I met years ago. Her eyes rove the room, and it seems there is someone who recognises her.

He is clad in all kinds of designer labels: Louis Vuitton at the top, a struggling Gucci belt across his taut bulge, and tightfitting pants. His loafers flash Lacoste and his watch blinds us all.

'Ah, Maggie, I knew I would see you again. How are you enjoying Lagos so far?'

'It's been great, thank you. Please meet my cousin, Bupe. She just came in from London today. Bupe, meet Bola Richards. I met him when I arrived here. We were on the same flight.'

'Ah, very nice. I hope you sef you don't have wedding ring like dis your cousin here.'

'No way! Single and free to mingle.' I wriggle my fingers in the air.

'And you Maggie. Is your husband here?' he looks around, 'I mean, is he physically here in this building?'

'He's in Zambia actually.'

'Ah, wonderful. In that case, would you ladies like to join my friend and me? He's also just come in from Dubai. We are seated outside.'

'Sure!' Maggie and I both say, and we snake our way through the bopping bodies. It's unlike her to be so eager to hang with someone she doesn't know.

Outside, he summons us to a table and pulls our chairs out for us. 'I think he has gone to take a call, but he should be back soon. Maggie, you never told me where you are from?'

I notice my cousin hesitate. 'I'm from Zambia,' she says, 'but my dad is from here.'

'So, you are Nigerian then?'

'Well, yes, I guess.'

He laughs. 'Look at dis bobo now. Don't you know that just one small drop of Naija blood makes you a full Nigerian? In fact, your children's children will forever be Naija, oh.'

We all laugh.

His friend appears and glides towards us; forming like a sand dune. He looks like a desert angel in white dishdasha and chocolate brown boat shoes. He smiles beautifully and his teeth flash perfection. His brown eyes dance beneath his ghutra. He has a pope's nose.

He says something to me, and I don't respond. I gawk back at him.

'Bupe!' Maggie calls me out. 'Forgive my cousin. She travelled from London, and it's her first time here. What's your name?'

'Fahed. Fahed Al Hinai.'

I watch him shake Maggie's hand. He turns to shake mine. His is warm, and soft, and oh-so large. He smells of humus, olives, coconut oil, and something else. Allure. I thought the Burj Khalifa was a building, but this lad right here, damn.

'Fahed is like you Maggie. His father is Omani, and his mother is Hausa. But we will still call him Fine-Naija boy.' He laughs.

'Wow, that must make you one badass businessman.' I take a sip of my drink.

'Actually, yes, you could say that. It is to Allah I give the glory. You two are very beautiful. Any relation?' Fahed's words are cryptic. Northern Nigerian with a Middle Eastern influence.

'Yes, we are cousins.' Maggie and I say this at the same time.

'Well, what can I say? Fine feathers make fine birds.'

'Fine words butter no parsnips, kind sir.' I'm blushing, beaming profusely.

'But the faint heart never won a fair lady.'

My tongue goes back into a knot, and I look at his golden brown skin some more.

'Oya, look at these two, turning a good night into a Shakespearian play. Would you ladies like some champagne?'

Into the night, the four of us enjoy each other's company.

Fahed suggests we go with him to his partner's house. He's looking after it while he's back in Dubai. Downstairs, we leave in his Aston Martin, and I can't believe Maggie hasn't protested yet. She's actually succumbed to a flute of bubbly, and she's been dancing like there's no tomorrow. I think about Jerome, but I look at Fahed's face, and I'm sure this must be love. We get into a car each. Maggie with Bola. Me with Fahed. I didn't know that Aston Martin leather could be so seductive.

At the house, massive gates tower over us, and they open after Fahed speaks into an intercom. We follow a winding driveway to a chateau. My head is spinning, and I know we shouldn't be here, but Maggie and I have tossed caution to the wind, maybe because we feel safe knowing we're together.

We stand in the lobby, our feet planted to the ground, and we look up at the massive crystals on the chandelier hovering above us. A butler stands at the foot of the stairs with a blinded falcon perched on his gloved arm.

'Let me show you something interesting.' Fahed takes us to an elevator.

To our surprise, its numbers begin at minus three. Underground floors? We should panic. Instead we're giggling like we're back in high school. The elevator descends.

Its doors open, and cold, clammy air meets our skin. As we step out, we are handed oversized fur coats by another graceful butler. Champagne is served to us on a tray, and we walk onto an icy landscape. A transparent baby grand piano twinkles on a white stage. Blue lighting softens the room and makes the piano gleam. We sit on regal chairs, and I get silly. Being in Fahed's presence has got me acting like a child again.

'Well, I ain't never seen nuffin like this before. Like ever.'

'My boss has a passion for wildlife. Will show you shortly. For now, sit back, relax, and just enjoy yourself.'

Bola strokes the thick hairs of his arms and leans in towards my cousin. 'Eh, Maggie, you see now. This is what you call first class sef. Iz a shame dat you have dat your husband in Zambia. He is lucky that I am a man of high moral standard. I would love to tek good care of you. Make you my second wife. I know first class when I see it.' He smacks his lips. He looks like he could do with a Christian Dior bib the way he's drooling over her.

The lights around us dim, and bright white light floods a stage behind a glass screen. Swear down on my mother's life, a real-life polar bear slides onto the ice! It does! Slowly on its bottom, while it turns around to face us.

Maggie and I gasp.

Fahed looks at me. I don't care that he can see me with my mouth-wide-open face. Hands glued to my flushed cheeks, the only sound I let out is a chain of explosive yelps. Light jazz plays and the bear appears to move to the music. Invisible hands throw twisting sardines from metal pails at the side of the stage. The beast pauses to eat.

'Meet Rudy!' Fahed says with a sparkle in his eyes.

'What in the world does your partner do? He's got a polar bear in the middle of Lagos?' We sink back into our seats, rapt.

'We are in the business of energy. All kinds of energy in developing countries. Most of our investments are in hydroelectric power. Me in particular, I have a focus on rural areas.'

'Have you ever considered investing in Zambia?' Maggie asks. 'We have an average GDP growth of about 6 per cent with 40 per cent of water resources in the southern African region. About 6,000 megawatts of unexploited hydropower potential is sitting with us—untouched. We have so many waterfalls and the potential to supply energy to a lot of our neighbours. We have eight neighbours I should point out.'

Bola claps his hands. 'I knew it! I have an eye for diamonds. Listen to dis woman. Beauty and brains in one!'

'That is quite impressive. I would like to visit someday.' Fahed turns to look at me.

'You are always welcome,' I say, forgetting the fact I haven't been there in almost ten years.

Suddenly, the low music skips. It spurts out the same notes repeatedly and stops. An explosive roar fills the room. It permeates every part of my body. Maggie and I scream, clutching one another. Our voices make the bear more agitated. He paws heavily at the glass barrier. The small boys with the pails of flicking sardines scatter in all directions.

Fahed's face is ashen, but he holds out his hand to me. Bola has long since climbed under his chair, and Maggie is wrenching my arm. We dart over to the baby grand. My fingers hover above the keys. I begin to play. My index fingers together first tap F and G and move outwards, striking the keys to the only piece I know: 'Tiyende Pamodzi.'

Rusty at first, but soon I'm performing with gusto. I play and play, my eyes sealed tight. Maggie sings the words. By some miracle, Rudy calms. He sits back on his haunches and lowers himself slowly to the floor like he's ready to sleep. After some minutes, the calmed bear is led away.

The lads take us back to our hotel, apologising profusely. Bola seems to have forgotten all the machoism he had before the event. He is a giddy silent. Jerking with a twist to look over his shoulder any time a sound is made.

'Come to Zambia for a good old-fashioned game drive,' I say to Fahed. He kisses my cheek ever so gently.

'Good night.'

Maggie and I jump into my bed, leaving the curtains wide open. The Lagos skyline blinks. We are still shaken but can't stop laughing. We lie on our backs, enjoying the softness of the duck down duvet.

'I swear I can't remember the last time I had so much fun!' I snort.

'I have something to tell you, sis.'

Maggie pauses, then says, 'I'm going to have a baby.'

'What? That's amazing, Maggie. Terrence must be over the moon!'

'I haven't told him yet. We still have a lot of issues to work out.'

'Like what, Maggie? He would give anything to make sure you're happy. You know this. I mean, remember how you were certain that he wouldn't marry you, and he went on a crusade against anyone in his family who would say otherwise? He's always stood up for you.'

'Well, it's no fairy tale ending either.'

'I know, cuz. But he's your friend. He loves you.'

The room is quiet. I hold her hand. Our fingers clasp into one fist. A tear rolls down the side of my face, but she doesn't see it.

'Guess what? I'm up too.'

'What? When? Are you and Jerome going to get married? Are you going to get a job?'

'I really don't have a clue yet. I want a child that has all his grandparents there. I want to be married when I have a baby. But I now know that I can't be married to Jerome. He's still a kid himself. And lately, I think I may want to live in Zambia too. I can't raise a baby in a bedsit, Maggie. We have land so vast that we can't see where it starts and stops. To do that to this child would be criminal. Jerome will never understand that, though.'

'Well, you can always come back home you know. It's always going to be there, whatever you decide. And we're here for you – it's what family does right?'

'And you Maggie?'

'I needed to see my dad before I could bring a child into this world.' Her eyes light up. 'It's going so well, Bupe. It feels like dream. I think I'm ready to do this. I'm ready to have this baby.'

CHAPTER 25

MAGGIE OLUWASEUN AYOMIDE
LAGOS, NIGERIA 2017

AFTER MUCH PROTEST FROM my father, Bupe and I head back to the mainland to visit Agege market. Youngharry is our designated chaperone. Bupe huffs about getting a cab, but I insist on public transport, longing to fully appreciate my second home. We get on a three-wheeler to the bus stop, and finally onto wooden plank seats inside a danfo. The conductor looks like a wind vane, hanging out of the bus while it moves. I ask him nicely to please come inside where it is safe, and they all laugh at me. Bupe rolls her eyes, and Youngharry apologises on my behalf.

'E no be from hia!' His teenage voice croaks, undecided on whether it is soprano or alto. "Oho!" They chorus as we swerve to the left.

The conductor shouts over the wind, right foot threatening to graze the tar, 'If she no be from hia, mek she dey watch! Abi, JJC you no wan mek I shadow my passenger well?' He laughs. I give him my most charming smile, clueless to what he has said.

My battering eyelids have no effect on him.

'Abeg, if you be JJC, mek sure sey you get change o, because I go just join you with person.' This time Youngharry checks his tattered wallet, and thankfully there is change. We won't have to be encumbered by another changeless stranger.

I whisper to Youngharry, or at least I think I do, as our ride becomes bumpier by the second, 'What is JJC?'

The whole bus shouts the answer, 'Johnnie Just Come Oh!'

Bupe joins in their laughter, and she's pointing at me like she's one of them. She covers her mouth like she's dissing me. I suck my teeth and roll my eyes, 'abeg, wettin be yours again?'

*

The market abounds with people and colours – bright red tomatoes by the mountain. Giant snails, their shells point upwards to the sky as if on offer to the gods. Buckets of shea butter blocks soak in water. Open air meat markets with bush meat skinned to their hooves and tail, set out on their backs displaying gutted belly and fresh insides, ready for inspection. Doli cubes, gingers, melon seeds, glistening black fish curled up in the positions from which they drew their last watery breath. The sounds of women calling out for people to see their merchandise. Grinders carefully putting measured contents in their funnels to produce ground crayfish or egusi seed. I have never seen so much food in one place. How is it possible for hunger to exist side-by-side with such abundance?

Bupe is taking pictures of everything with her phone, and it's beginning to annoy me. I would rather not attract the attention of being a foreigner in a place that is supposed to be my country.

We cross the railway tracks to visit the cloth-selling side of the market. After a few rows, I find a stall with a good ankara and lace selection. The orange-faced lady with pitch black lipstick and coral beads across her generous bosom is happy when I give her my withered Naira. She smiles a wide smile, revealing pale gums and yellow teeth. My merchandise is folded neatly and handed to me in a plastic bag. She begins to heave, and her eyes roll backwards. She dances in a hop and a step and begins to slap the notes I have given her against her patterned wares, repeating, 'Opun market for me! Opun market for me!'

Youngharry grabs our wrists, and we walk away quickly. I am happy with my purchase, but afraid that I may have been pulled into that woman's diabolical world. I cross my heart and ask God for forgiveness if I have given my money to a witch.

Like a baby who forgets easily, I find another lady selling beautiful earthenware pots. I know that I cannot buy them to carry back to Lusaka, but they are so alluring, I stop to ask how much they are. I find the courage to try some basic Yoruba.

'Eelo ni eleyi?' I ask.

A woman of substantial build sits on a low wooden stool. She looks at me intensely, like she's trying to remember me from another time. She doesn't answer. She glares deeply into my soul. Uncomfortable, I hope I have not said the wrong word to insult her. I lick my parched lips nervously and try again.

'Eelo ni Ma?'

Abruptly, she bursts into throaty laughter. It is so loud, it echoes, like she is sitting at the bottom of a drum. She gracelessly slaps the back of her neck and wipes her sweaty brow. She says I sound like oyinbo. She calls her friends to hear my accent. 'Come an' see dis one oh! E no be from hia!'

I laugh uncomfortably, but Bupe asks them if we can all take a selfie. They dissolve with more laughter and plenty of excitement. We all pose for her Instagram photo. Short, tall, light, dark, fat, thin, scarified, and plain-faced, we are all smiling, united in the moment for this one photograph before she beams it to the world.

'E se!' I say, and I leave the shiny-cheeked lady with a

decent tip. As I place the Naira in her hand, she grips my arm. I panic, remember Dad's warnings about kidnap.

The intensity in her round eyes returns. Her voice becomes low and gruff.

'You no be ordinary gel!! You get big big destiny talents from many many places. Mek you ask God – he go show you how! Hmm bet, you have to work together. You an' diz brown gel, diz fine one. Together.'

Taken aback, I finally find my voice again.

'E se Ma!' I walk away.

'God bless you oh!' She waves, still laughing. 'Big big madam dat one,' she shouts to her friends.

*

I see Bupe off on a cab to her hotel and go back to my grandparents' house. I offer to read a story to my grandfather while the nurse takes my grandma for her bath. He enjoys the book because it is set in his village. He won't let me finish because every familiar landmark mentioned makes him jump with excitement. I realise that we won't get past the third paragraph.

'I know, let's play a game of tic-tac-toe,' I say.

'XO?' he responds, asking the air.

I pull out a blank sheet of paper from my diary and draw two parallel lines down and two across. I place a big X at the centre and tell him to go for it. I pass him the pen.

His lower lip begins to quiver, and he becomes agitated. The corners of his mouth gather saliva. His eyes become slits of suspicion.

'What are you trying to make me do?'

'What do you mean, Grandpa? It's a game. Look here. We have to make a row of X's, in your case O's, and then you win!' I'm smiling, hoping to bring him back because I sense that he has retreated far into his mind and is nowhere near us.

'I will not sign anything! Anything. Do you hear me?' He raises his voice.

'Grandp—'

'Don't call me that! Take it away! Not until my secretary goes through it, and my wife approves, I am not signing a damn thing! You want to come here with the same buccaneering spirit as your father? Until you have us at our beam-ends, you will not rest? Eh? You think I do not see the two of you conniving, taking trips to my house? I hear you planning my death in the corridors!'

I try to keep calm – remind myself that he is not OK. But the room spins.

'Get out! Get out, you bottom feeder!' He flings a pillow at me, and I run.

CHAPTER 26

BUPE KOMBE
LAGOS, NIGERIA, 2017

'BUPE! THIS IS ABISOLA. Your cousin is on her way to you right now, and she's very upset. I'll be at the hotel before her, but if she gets there first, make sure to keep her with you.'

'What happened?'

'I'll explain later.'

I jump out of my giant white bed and make a dash for the shower. Maggie has been so happy here, and her dad seems to have reassured her of his love for her. What could have upset her? I brush my hair, sweep it into a bun, and change into a pair of shorts and a vest before I head to the lobby to wait.

Downstairs, I inform the portly receptionist of the impending arrival of my cousin. She rolls her eyes at my dramatic instruction. I wait. Feeling parched, I decide to slip to the restaurant for a drink when I spot Uncle Abisola. He has his back to me. He's hunched over, full attention on the phone in the palm of his hand, and as I approach him, I see her.

She's a Botox beauty whose face looks struck flat by an iron. Her voice whines and needles. She is complaining, mostly in French, partly in English. I'm about to turn around and go back to the buffet but then my uncle takes her off video puts the phone to his ear.

'Charleen, Charleen, calm down. I'll be back soon … I know, but I can't leave her here by herself… yes, I know, but the grandparents are also not doing well enough to be with her on their own. Oui, ma cherie, I understand. But you know the deal already. They won't let me inherit anything unless they see her. So, let me just manage this, and I'll be back home soon. Eh? Yes, honey, that's right. I will be home soon, and we can put this behind us.'

He puts down his phone and leans back to straighten out his shirt.

'Abisola Ayomide! My mum was right!' I feel my face alight with rage. He swerves around to look at me.

'How dare you address me like that!'

'I heard your entire conversation. I can't believe you would do this to Maggie!'

'What do you know about anything? No one is perfect OK, not even me, so don't stand there and judge me. Isn't it enough I brought you here?'

'You did not.'

'Well, whatever. You people are not so perfect either. None of them helped me and Stella when we were having trouble. My daughter was taken away from me and no one said anything. A whole family was cut off from each other, and in usual Kombe style, your people just watched it happen. Take a look in the mirror, all of you. You like to marry cooks' daughters and your forefathers killed their wives by fucking entertainers, a rhumba star, for crying out loud! You all stand there, judging me for one mistake I made so long ago!'

My face is so hot, my tears sting.

'She loves you, Abisola. So much that her entire life is on hold. She's been waiting for you ever since you left. She won't even start a family because she's so scared of going through that deep a loss again.'

He takes off his glasses to wipe his eyes. 'Yes, I failed

once, a long time ago. I will not let her or you, or anyone come here, to my home, and remind me of something that happened so many decades ago. Maybe it's better we go back to how things were before. I'll leave this afternoon, and you can tell her for me. I think it's best that she doesn't return to Lagos either.' He stands, slapping his serviette on the table. He's in a hurry to leave.

In spite of myself, I reach for him. 'Abisola, no! Please come back. Please! I'll pretend I never heard a thing.'

But he is gone. He slithers out of the building like a snake shedding its skin. He leaves it all behind.

I wait for Maggie, and I hope that she will forgive me. Did I do it? Should I have just shut up and closed my big mouth?

I sit in the lobby all day. I watch people walk in and out. Being transferred from one world to another. Darkness begins to fall, and my spirit sinks along with the sunset. Finally, she walks in. A sweaty mess. Her eyes puffy, her jeans filthy.

I take her hand, and we go up to my room. She has a long shower and asks room dining to bring her up an apple smoothie. She sits at the desk in her towelled gown. Her eyes are on the phone. I kneel next to her and whisper.

'He's gone, Maggie.'

'I know. He sent me a message.'

'I'm so sorry.'

'Me too. I'm so sorry to myself for not having loved myself enough before. I'm not going to live for him anymore. I have someone else to think of now.' She puts her hand to her belly, and she rubs it gently.

'Really?' I sit up. 'Are you going to have it, Maggie?'

'Yes, I will,' she sounds drained.

'It's time to really live. I'm married to a great guy, but I've had all these walls around me, it's no wonder he can't reach me.'

'Now that's the spirit. Maggie, you are so smart, and loving, and organised. You make a wonderful human being, are a fantastic wife, and will be a great mother. You've had so much faith in God, and He's done it for you. Abisola has his own judgement to deal with. But don't let him ruin yours. Did you hear that lady in the market? Bola the other night? You are a formidable force, Maggie. You've got to believe it.'

She cries into my shoulder, and I cry too. I get on to the bed and sit cross-legged.

'You should see me and Jerome. It's like I don't even exist anymore. And you know what? My mum is right. She always has been. He's a wastrel of a man. He is who is he is, I guess, and that's cool, but I don't have to be responsible for changing his life.'

'Why did you go back, though? After we finished school, I was so sure you'd move on.'

'I guess I just always wanted to feel insulated, like Mum and Dad, you know? In their own vacuum and all of that. Lovers since they were kids? It's the only picture I've ever had of love, and I felt if I didn't have it with Jerome, then I might miss it forever. And after school, in my own way, I was ready to punish them for sending me so far away.'

'Well, after the way you looked at Fahed, my darling, I think your spell has been broken.'

I cover my face with a pillow, and I breathe out heavily, 'Yes, maybe.'

'Do you think Grandma Margaret died because she was an alcoholic, or was my dad just making it up?'

'I don't know, Maggie. Uncle Abs seemed to think it was because of an affair Grandpa had with some rhumba dancer.'

'What? Did he say that?'

I nod my head. 'Maybe that's why Grandpa has always been so sad. Can you imagine having to live your life wondering if it was your fault? That your wife became an alcoholic and lost her life? Generations of a broken family because of you?'

'A lifetime of regret here is as good as an eternity of fire in hell.'

My phone rings. Dad's voice is flustered on the line. 'Girls, you have to head to Lusaka on the next flight. Your grandfather. He's taken a turn for the worst. We're not sure he's going to make it through the week. Make sure to leave tomorrow, and we will drive to Chinsali the day after.'

Maggie tries to call her mother, but all she gets is a standard recording message. 'The number you have dialled is not in use. Please try again later.'

CHAPTER 27

MAGGIE OLUWASEUN AYOMIDE
LAGOS, NIGERIA, 2017

ON THE WAY TO the airport, Bupe tries to cheer me up, and we make a last stop at Mr Biggs. I order fried chicken and jollof rice with moin-moin to go. I unwrap the foil of my pasty brown moin-moin wondering if I will get salmon or a boiled egg at the centre. I cut it in half, slowly, wondering why I always have a need to remove layers of things already in place. Why did I come here? I look around to see colourful couples and families coming from church dressed in matching lace and aso-oke. They hold hands and carry flashy Bibles. They eat the same food and speak the same language. The sons look just like their dads and the daughters kiss their mothers.

In the centre of the moin-moin is a firmly boiled egg. I don't eat much of it because I know I would rather have had salmon. And besides, there is a guava-sized lump in my throat. My heart is breaking all over again.

Why did I come here?

Through Murtala Muhammed International Airport, the personnel ask me to give them some money, a 'Small Sunday', which I don't have.

'Next time I will make sure to fly on Monday because I have no more Naira left.' They do not laugh with me.

Uncle Tayo and his old-man friend see us through to the check-in desk. We hug to say goodbye; again.

'Whatever happened with you and your father, please remember that the rest of the family still loves you. His actions should not affect our relationship with you. Please stay in touch with your grandparents, with me.'

I nod my head and hug him. 'Thanks, Uncle T.'

He hands me a plastic bag. 'I know it's an inconvenience to have to put it in your suitcase now, but your grandmother asked for you to have this.'

In the bag is coral beaded jewellery for my head and neck, some cloth, and a musty old Eleanor looking up at me as she lies on top of some heavy books. Uncle Tayo's old-man friend is so excited to get a hug goodbye, and he holds on to me for a second too long.

The man checking our boarding passes inspects my passport thoroughly. He licks his thick fingers to turn the pages. He analyses each stamp he sees. Malaysia. South Africa. Togo. Kenya. He looks at me and looks at its cover. The golden Zambian coat of arms gleams.

'Is this name not from here?' He traces an invisible line under my name with his wet finger, Margaret Oluwaseun Ayomide.

'Yes, it is, sir.'

'So why is this passport Zambian?'

'Because that is where my mother is from. I live there. I'm from there.'

'But your father has named you. Isn't it his blood which you take? And this is the first time you are coming here?'

He hands back the well-thumbed passport, looking at me over his spectacles. Before I can answer, I'm dismissed.

'Next please!'

I cry all the way back to the plane while Bupe bites her nails. Airports. I hate them.

CHAPTER 28

GRANDMOTHER MARGARET
LUSAKA, ZAMBIA, 1967

MRS MARGARET KOMBE PERCHED upright in the backseat of a large black Impala as her chauffer drove her to her Woodlands home. To the naked eye, the suburb was quiet and still. Perfectly dressed cadets in uniform guarded the gates of the large homes. High-beamed roofs distanced themselves from onlookers, hidden by thickets of palm trees, conifers, and frangipanis. Just a few years before, she would come across from the township with her children on foot, every Sunday after church. The baby would be safely tucked into the brown speckled chitenge on her back while the older two would be a few steps ahead of her, taking it all in with a silent reverence they had gleaned from their father.

'I will do everything in my power to ensure that our children grow up in Woodlands.' He promised her repeatedly.

'You will have distinguished guests from around the world, and you will serve them crumpets and tea in our indoor courtyard,' her husband would say to her. His head resting on his large palm while he stroked the head of the nursing baby at her bosom, the older children snoring next to them on their thin mattress. His eyes glistened bright in the paraffin-lit room.

The car stopped for a group of teenagers crossing the road from the Convent Girls School. She watched them laugh and talk to each other, in no particular hurry. The Convent would have been a wonderful place for Stella. Her eyes grew smaller at the thought of her children.

The driver handed her a note from his boss. She glanced at the familiar cursive writing, aware that it would read identically to all the others. His voice rolled in her ears.

> Bana CJ,
> There is a pressing matter in the Congo of which my presence is urgently required. I hope that you travelled back safely from Chinsali, and that, aba fyashi, balifye bwino. I should be back after a week. The house staff is at your beck and call, and I have informed the office that they are to ensure you are well catered for. Shalenipo no mutende—

Gingerly, she placed the note back into its stiff envelope. She shredded it into tiny strips and stuffed her handbag with them. She exchanged a quick glance in the rearview mirror with her chauffer. He looked away briskly for making such a faux pas. Was that sympathy she noted in his soft nod?

The car pulled into their arched driveway. Its gurgling water fountain made her pull on the fingers of her gloves – suddenly they were too tight. The fountain was a lion's head spewing clear liquid out of its mouth at all hours of the day – what could possibly be attractive about that?

Her car door was opened for her, and she walked into her silent house. Her perfect oil-painted family beamed at her – they were set in the finest gold frame bought from an antique store in the heart of London.

Her maid curtsied low, asking what time she would like her dinner served. Margaret assured her that she would ring the bell when she was ready to eat. She looked at the oil painting and remembered how they had two rushed days with the children that weekend, and how she fought with Charles because she wanted them all to wear a chitenge ensemble she had worked so hard on.

She began up the stairs, allowing the cold wood of the banister to lead her to her room – to her secret place. She paused to look at the perfectly placed reception chairs, contrasting well against her silk woven Persian rugs. Floor to ceiling curtains, hooked in equal semi–circles by frayed golden tie backs. She rubbed her temple, wishing for her head to hurt no more.

Images of Stella tore through her. The young girl dashing upstairs to her room to return with her easel and charcoal, planting it before her.

'Here, tell me again, Mother, slowly, what you said, and maybe I can draw signs that make it easier for us to understand each other! You've got to let go of that jungle talk. You're not in Chinsali anymore! And while we're on the topic, why can't we go to the Caribbean for the summer like the Fosters?'

Margaret closed her eyes, wondering where it had all gone so terribly wrong. The Bemba say all children that share a pillow in the womb of their mother are eternally connected. It is a gift given to family by the Creator, a bond that can never be broken.

But what happens when the centre does not hold?

PART III

CHAPTER 29

MAGGIE OLUWASEUN AYOMIDE
CHINSALI, ZAMBIA, 2017

THERE IS SILENCE IN the car. We are a convoy of three vehicles: Uncle CJ, Aunt Jasmine, and Bupe in one, and Uncle Kabaso and Terrence in the next. I am with Mum. She hasn't spoken to me since my return.

'How is he?'

I shrug my shoulders and shake my head.

'And Mummy and Daddy?' She twists the copper ring on her middle finger.

'They are fine, although Grandpa doesn't have his memory all the time. He comes and goes, if you know what I mean.' I look at the palm fronds in the valley as we drive along Danger Hill. When I was little, tales were told of how this area was lion infested. This part of the journey was always full of terrifying stories. I try to remember them so that I can replace the last image I have of the demon that unleashed itself through my grandfather. Her question brings me back to reality.

'So, did you find it?'

'Find what, Mum?'

'What you think you were looking for?' I choose not to answer.

She clicks her tongue and mumbles something under her breath. She turns to face her side of the window. The mound of her smoothly shaved head stares back at me.

'It's not my fault, Mum! You chose him, not me.'

She turns around, astounded. 'What?'

'Yes, you heard me. If you had been responsible enough to find a decent human being for a partner, maybe we wouldn't be in this mess.'

'There has been no mess. You went and made it all by yourself. I told you to forget about him. He is an adult. He's not going to suddenly change now. People don't change. Not for you, not for anybody!'

I burst into tears, and I expect her to keep shouting, but in a swift sweep, she pulls me close to her. She embraces me in her bosom, and I release all my pain. 'He's my father. It's not possible for me to just forget him and move on. He's the only father I have and that means he's mine, both good and bad. I need you to understand that.'

'I know, I know. I'm sorry, Maggie. I don't know how else to protect you from this – this pain.'

'You can't, Mum. I feel betrayed, rejected, not just in this moment but from a lifetime's worth of not having him here. I need you to be my mother, my shoulder to cry on, just this once, Mum, please.'

'OK, honey. I'm sorry. Calm down. It will be alright. I promise. I'm here for you.'

*

After a rocky uphill drive to the house – a feat even for any 4×4 – we park the cars and get to the porch. A group of volunteers eagerly offload our luggage, and we stretch our bodies like freed rubber bands. After almost 1,000 kilometres from Lusaka, plus overnight flights with connections for most of us, we are all spent.

Bana Mpundu, my mother's cousin or sister by customary tradition, leads us into the house. She has looked after Grandfather since he moved back here. Her twins are the same age as Bupe and I. Inswa – flying ants – dot the sky as the smell of imminent rainfall hangs over the mountains. They bump against the fluorescent tubes repeatedly, giving a tapping sound mixed with a muted buzz. On any other occasion, they would have been caught and de-winged to make a quick snack on a pan.

Bana Mpundu says the doctor has left, and under strict instructions, none of us should spend more than ten minutes in his room. She puts her index finger to her lips, and her shadow flickers tall against the wall. The uncles go in first, then Mum and Aunty Jasmine. Finally, Bupe and I hold hands, and we walk along the hall to his bedroom. We pass a number of elderly people whom we kneel to greet. They look at us with sorrowful eyes as though he has already gone.

His headboard looks like it fell out of the 1960s – it still has a fixed in radio in it. Grandmother Margaret's portrait sits next to his black, leather-bound Bible. She is smiling and has a round afro, immortalized by the skilled camera person who took the photograph.

The pink of Grandfather's soles pop from under his blanket. He is too tall for his own bed. The sound of his breathing is heavy and laboured. A metal tank sits next to him, and the mask above his mouth and nose alternates from vapour-filled to clear. A long pole with a bag of fluid has tubes connected to his left arm. Drip. Drip. Drip. Bupe and I hold hands, and we pray for him, remembering our misty day at the waterfalls. Our special time with him. 'Tata,' we say, 'please don't go yet. We still need you. They still need you.'

Bana Mpundu later shows each of us the self-contained rooms that have been prepared for us. Now that I am married, I have a room with a double bed. Its frayed curtains have faded rectangles in their middles from the light of the sun. The once silky Persian rugs are worn through to bare threads. Our side tables are classic pieces of handmade furniture in desperate need of repair. However, they stand proud on their wooden lion paws and curly handles. A painting on the wall hangs crooked. I am drawn to it and reach out to straighten it. The primary colours and soft strokes are seductive as is the woman drawing water at the river against a backdrop of shadowed, hanging forest.

My husband, who has arrived just moments ago, checks for snakes and creepy-crawlies with a crooked hanger he found in the empty wardrobe. We sit on either side of the old bed and its worn-out springs cave into a low hammock in its middle. It rolls us both down the centre, forcing us to face each other. We burst out laughing.

'I missed you,' he says.

'I missed you too,' I whisper.

'I'm so sorry about your grandfather. I know it's almost time. I was an idiot not to come to Lagos with you.' I put my finger to his lips.

'Can we start all over again?' he asks.

I look into his eyes. This time with a new perspective on longevity. On love and the ugliness of beauty.

'We are going to have a baby,' I whisper.

He pulls me in, and we breathe deeply into the crooks of each other's necks. A new lease on love.

'We are always running away or fighting,' I stutter.

'What did you say?' he asks.

'I don't want to be called "the one that fled".'

He laughs into my neck. 'What have you done with my wife? What are you talking about?'

'Please don't give up on me. I don't know how to do this love thing without feeling like it's all going to be over.'

'What do you mean?'

'I don't know how to do families with happy endings, relying on others, and all that stuff. It's like I'm not supposed to be here; married and happy; like I'll be discovered for a fraud.'

'An imposter?' He laughs. 'Honey, I love you unconditionally; just the way you are and exactly how you were made.'

I pull away so that I can look into his eyes.

'I don't want to have children if they are going to go through what I did.'

'Now that, my darling, is up to us. Both of us.'

CHAPTER 30

MAGGIE OLUWASEUN AYOMIDE
CHINSALI, ZAMBIA, 2017

UNCLE CJ LOOKS LIKE the grandmother I never got to meet, a striking resemblance to the stunning lady in the pictures. It is strange. The last in the series of paintings and photographs of them all together as a family end when Uncle CJ and Mum must have been teenagers. A gold framed oil painting hangs in the sitting room, looking like it could be sold at Sotheby's – Grandfather with his arm around Grandmother and his other hand on Uncle CJ's shoulder, Grandmother's hand on my mother's shoulder, and a little Uncle Kabaso in the middle. The men wear suits and bow ties, Grandmother is in a ball gown, and my mother wears a floral dress with a sash at her waist. Like a river flowing gradually, from babies to toddlers, school-going, black and white studio shots, this frame, then nothing! As if blocked by a dam, the visual portrayal of a family's growth ends; abruptly.

Uncle CJ thumbs through Grandpa's Rhodesian law book collection while Aunt Jasmine speaks softly to a group of village women who have gathered outside. One of the twins acts as her translator. Little children play around her, and she kisses their faces. She makes Bana Mpundu give them bowls of brown millet porridge. Her crowd seems to be growing and her speeches seem to be getting fervent. Uncle CJ looks up to watch her from the window, and I see his lips curl into a smile. His love for his wife is the kind you can feel. It has a physical quality about it, like a country you can actually go to, with its own civilisation and infrastructure, its own language and history, rituals and rites, except they've reserved entry for themselves. He puts his book away and walks outside to join her.

One of the little boys has a ball made of bound plastics, sealed carefully by heat, probably from the flame of a candle. The outer plastic has a defaced Rambo; it's a mystery who makes the plastic bags printed with the serious pose of Sylvester Stallone. Uncle CJ asks the boy if he can play, and soon a full football match is going while the women open up to Aunt Jasmine and lay their burdens before her.

In the kitchen that night, Uncle CJ reveals his secret stash of rum. Aunt Jasmine comes out in a well-wrapped chitenge, her complexion and eyes sorely out of place – a focus for many of the visitors at the house. She collects a bucket of hot water and disappears into one of the bedroom wings.

Bupe goes outside to find a rock on the mountain with a good signal so she can call Jerome.

Uncle Kabaso comes in with his long, relaxed hair, tied back in a ponytail – his subtle make-up flawless.

'Can't you play it down even just for the next few days while we are here?' Uncle CJ asks.

'Play what down? You should count your lucky stars I didn't come with Pascale,' he retorts, rolling his eyes in a swoon.

'No, you should count your lucky stars mate – the two of you could be locked up, carrying on all willy nilly in these parts.'

Kabaso flicks his hand dismissively.

'Rum?' Uncle CJ asks.

'No, I'll have a Mosi, thank you. Why don't we sit outside so we can have a fag as well?'

'Smartest thing you've said all day.'

On the patio, Bana Mpundu lights paraffin lanterns.

'These lanterns always remind me of Mum, you know,' Uncle Charles says.

'Koloboi,' he says in an English accent.

Kabaso lights a cigarette and retreats into his thoughts. 'Who's going to stay here when the old man goes?' he asks, facing the thick forest that climbs upwards into the mountains. The sound of crickets and frogs fill the night air. No one speaks.

A half dozen ladies cook on mbabulas spread along the grass, fanning their flames to grow their fires. One lady pivots her brazier from her shoulder at a full 360 degrees – around and around in a perfect circle into the night air with her right arm, her chitenge held up with her left hand. Sparks of blue and orange spit from the brazier as it settles. Her fire ready, she spoons beans into her pot.

'Maggie – where is your mother?' Uncle CJ asks.

'She'll be here. She's having her bath and checking on Grandpa.'

'So, do tell, how is your father? And of course, your grandmother Merlene? The most beautiful woman in the world?' He looks over his shoulder to make sure Aunt Jasmine is still out of sight. He smirks.

'Grandma is fine, just old now. Dad is Dad, I guess. The leopard doesn't change its spots.'

He laughs at the thought. 'Well, yes, Abs will be Abs, but you're going to be fine, love, I promise. I mean, just look at you. You have grown into a strong successful woman, and we're very proud of you. And your grandad? How is he? I swear that man was one of the nicest people I ever knew.'

He drags his cigarette.

'Why don't you talk to Dad if you were so close?' I ask.

'It became complicated once he married my little sister, and even more so when they divorced. So, no, it's not my kind of tea party, if you know what I mean. Besides, that means I would have to be friends with his toad of wife.' We all burst out laughing.

'On a serious note, I feel that she could have done more to ensure that your relationship with him and their children was kept intact, but she's a selfish prat if you ask me.'

I shrug in nonchalant agreement. 'Uncle CJ, Daddy told me something strange when I was there.'

'What, love?' he looks at me with genuine concern.

'He said Grandma drowned in the swimming pool at home because she was an alcoholic? And he told Bupe that there was a rhumba dancer involved?'

He drags his cigarette deeply, its red glow extending for centimetres before he draws breath. Uncle Kabaso passes his palm over his sleek ponytail repeatedly, and his eyes are moist.

As if on cue, Mum walks in with Aunt Jasmine. They sense the tension that hides just behind the crickets and frogs' evening performance. The buzzing of mosquitoes adds a new dimension to the bush orchestra.

'He's had his bath and his bed has been turned over so that he doesn't get bedsores. Doc feels we may have to keep him on oxygen permanently from now on,' says Mum, always the serious one.

Terrence walks onto the patio to join us. His boots thud heavily on the patio floor. He chokes us as he's doused in mosquito repellent. Every inch of his skin covered. Everyone stares at him for a moment. 'Would you like some gloves and a hat as well then, ol' chap?' Uncle CJ asks.

As everyone cackles, Uncle CJ pours him some rum.

Aunt Jasmine takes a seat next to her sister-in-law, and Bupe finally returns from her phone call with puffy eyes. Her brow is furrowed, but when she catches my eye, she flashes a determined half smile. A secret nod, and I know she's OK.

'Have I missed something?' my mother asks.

Uncle CJ clears his throat.

'Stella, I find it ironic that you haven't spoken to me properly for all these years because I didn't tell you that

Mum had died – on Father's orders, might I add – and here I am all the way from London, on a veranda in Chinsali, and Maggie is asking me how, in fact, Mum died. You mean you haven't told her?'

'Hey, Ba Charlie, mister first born, you have no right to come here and tell me what to do, I've fended for this child by myself without that wretched friend of yours – singlehandedly – and where have you been, dear brother? Hmm? All these years? So, forgive me if I do not feel like I owe you an explanation on what I do or don't share with my daughter!

'Bana Mpundu – mpeniko red wine – ili mu pantry. No munkoyo ayini, Ba Si? Quickly!' she orders, her irritation evident. My husband squeezes my hand. He offers in a nervous voice to open the wine that arrives with Bana Mpundu and pours it for his mother-in-law.

'Well, what did you want me to do? You stopped talking to me, answering my letters – nothing!' Uncle CJ asks.

'I came home to pick up all the pieces. Me, the only girl in this whole damn family, and not even the oldest! When Dad was being held for over a year, who took care of the estate? When he finally came out with his health so deteriorated, and one eye lost when people would run the other way as I walked towards them where were you, big brother dearest? And as for you, Kabaso, being the kasuli is not an excuse to send your only parent the 'Lord of the Rings' trilogy when he is fresh out of prison and trying to get his life back together! Did you think Frodo and Gandalf were going to feed him? No! Get on a bloody plane and come see your father.'

Uncle Kabaso's face registers shock, and he is ready to come back, but he chooses not to. He keeps his index finger in the air while his other hand rests on his hip. He presses his lips together and shifts from foot to foot.

'That's enough!' Uncle CJ stands.

'You know Kabaso was struggling financially then – give him a break. And would Dad have taken lightly to his son coming home – gay? No offence, Kabaso. We're just speaking the truth here, it seems! So sanctimonious.' CJ mimics her with his hands held together as though in prayer.

'You left London like a thief in the night – literally! If it weren't for me and your sister-in-law, Maggie would have grown up with both you and Abs behind bars!'

My mother's lips retract into a straight line. She folds her arms tightly. She blinks fast and turns her face away from Uncle CJ. She has been pushed off her high horse and has fallen. Uncle CJ seems to have located her bête noir, and she looks into the night, seething.

'Where were you when I had not two pennies to rub together and Jasmine was being harassed by the police for her involvement with the Brixton Riots? Before they let her off on some flimsy line about "inadmissible evidence". Flying concords to New York on stolen money and borrowed time?' Everyone gasps.

Aunt Jasmine makes a fist and punches into the air – she smiles a naughty smile. Uncle Kabaso fans his face as though he can't take the heat. The argument continues back and forth like a tennis match.

'I'm pregnant!' shouts Bupe.

'What?' Everyone whips their heads towards her.

'Us too,' my husband and I say and smile. They swivel in our direction.

'Son, pour me another glass.' Mother gulps her drink. She pulls out her fan, which seems to extend magically from her wrist. Aunt Jasmine's face turns crimson. She looks at Bupe with shock, but I don't see disappointment, thankfully. She begins to ask her the when's and why's and they stand to hug.

Kabaso disappears inside to come out with his wireless speakers and plays Gregory Abbott.

'Remember when Bupe was terrified of his picture on the LP, but she could sing every word of "Shake You Down" when she was four?' he asks. 'All that makeup, conked hair, and eye contacts used to make her scream!'

Everyone laughs. Tensions ease.

'Midnight Train to Georgia' comes on next. Mum kisses Bupe first and then me. She gives a respectful clap of thanks to my husband while she kneels in her chitenge.

'Your grandmother, girls, was a formidable woman. I was too shallow and immature to see it when she was alive.' She sips her wine. 'She created a family even in the absence of your grandfather. Being married to a freedom fighter was not an easy thing to do in those days.

'Charles, I am so sorry for carrying such bitterness for so long, and I will try to forgive you. It hurt so much to not have been able to see her one last time, even if it was just for a moment in her coffin, and yet, you had that opportunity. By the time we returned from school, Dad had replaced her with that Congolese slut – and I mean that in every way. No paintings, no pictures, not her clothes, nothing!' She slams her wine glass on the table, turgid red pellets materialise on its wooden surface.

'And yes, I hated that you had gotten the chance to say goodbye. It was only after Fabiola ran away with another ex-president that he returned to his senses and gave our home any semblance of respect to Mum.' Kabaso is crying. Bupe too.

'So, how did she really die?' I ask.

Everyone is quiet again, for a long time.

'She died from grief, girls. Real, deep seated grief. I've always felt guilty for contributing to that,' Mum replies.

Kabaso finally speaks. 'We are all here now. Children, grandchildren, and great-grandchildren from the look of things. It's time to start over again. Stella, you have done an excellent job managing Dad's and your own political career. Raising Maggie by yourself – we wish we could rewind and be there, or in the same country, but we weren't. Charles, I can't imagine how hard it must have been to not be able to tell your own siblings only because Dad said so and to go through it alone.'

Before he can say his next sentence, Sam Cooke's soulful, hurting but hopeful voice fills the night-time air. 'This song makes me think of Dad all the time. "Change Gonna Come!"'

Mum says, 'Me too!'

They all agree on something finally. Everyone sings along, each one lost in individual memories of him as a father, a grandfather, and a politician. I breathe in the smoky smell of the munkoyo in my tin cup and chew the grainy bits, not sure how to control my emotions. Above all the emotions, hope rises, a hope that we do not repeat the same mistakes for the little heartbeats in our bellies.

At that moment, the row of women cooking on the fires begin a chain of whispers. The sound of cooking sticks and chopping boards comes to a halt. The crickets and frogs fall silent. Bana Mpundu is running through the glass house – we can see her. She's coming fast, but my mind plays the scene slowly. By the time she reaches Mum and Uncle CJ, we know.

The shrill wails of the house guests, the guardians of Grandfather's quarters, ring through the night.

He is gone – the great Charles Kombe.

Drums sound from the patio and the village responds. Amalila – war songs fill the air. They light up one by one – the huts hidden in the hills. Even though it is night, we see the bodies join as one, flickering kolobois in hand, walking towards the long bungalow atop the hill. Chinsali has lost a great one – again. By morning, the hills are filled with thousands of people, perching in trees, sitting on the grass, all forlorn. By afternoon the army rolls in and takes over. They build a tent for the mourners. Tremors ripple through the mountains as they blast into the rocks for his resting place. State preparations are in motion, choppers cut through the air, landing in rising clouds of dust. Red carpets are rolled out, cameras snap, and interviewers fill our home – he belongs to his country now, no more to us.

EPILOGUE

A WATER TANK SITS high on a bed of droopy, flamboyant flowers in blossom. The plant creeps all the way down the steel frame that holds it up. The tank is full to the brim, water pouring over and spilling to the ground. Two children splash in the swimming pool at the Woodlands home in Lusaka. We watch them, holding hands.

Charles is in the lobby mapping out the boundaries of the Chinsali farm while Jasmine hangs over his shoulder, asking for more space for her children's school.

Stella is on the phone, running her fingers through her thick dread locks. The wooden box with the domed carving sits next to her. It spills over with malachite jewellery. She is confirming the attendance of her fellow MPs for the upcoming launch of the eco-village and hydropower station in Chinsali.

Kabaso is watching the kids swim through a video call.

'Can you believe we are actually doing this?'

'I know, right? Fahed's people are calling for a telco in ten minutes.'

We look at the trucks lined up in the driveway, littered with potbellied men who chew on straw, waiting for tomorrow's journey. The vehicles are loaded with furniture – our future. We will leave at dawn for our new home in Chinsali. Our historical hotel and art gallery will be showcased during the opening.

Sampa the Great's 'Final Form' blares from one of the trucks.

'Are you ladies finally ready to claim your birthright?' Jasmine creeps up behind us, her beautiful face framed in an aqua turban. Her olive green eyes twinkle at us. She holds two glasses of champagne in hand, her eyebrows raised.

We look towards the trees because they begin to speak to each other. Soft ripples at first, but then strong whispers begin, followed by the sound of distant laughter. We smile upwards, listening. We can hear them both. Reunited, forgiven, and healed. They are happy, and they speak of country. Of family.

'We are as ready as we can ever be.'

The little girls come out of the pool, and shivering, they both call out, 'Mama! Mama! Look!' They take a few steps back and run forwards, folding their knees to their chins. They jump into the water, bottoms first.

END

ACKNOWLEDGEMENTS

It takes a village, so in no particular order a most sincere thank you is due to:

My husband Gregory Kalulu Banda – for his love and his extraordinary ability to let me disappear into places no one else can see. For helping me create Bupe's world in Brixton, and keeping our kids happy when I needed to 'go in'. My mother Chileshe Kapwepwe for her unshakeable faith in the gifts of her children, her warm home and constant pearls of wisdom – for always leading by example. My mothers, for I was not born to one. Aunty Mulenga Kapwepwe – for making me accountable and reading some of the earliest and roughest drafts. For the countless meetings over tea and the invaluable references. For inspiring me to create. Aunty Chilufya Kapwepwe for enduring my endless questions about Chinsali and life before Independence. Aunty Sampa Kapwepwe for always making me feel at home in England.

My father, Anthony Omokhodion for his unconditional love and support, sending me proverbs at all hours of the night and carting me around Lagos, checking if I've eaten and all of that mushy stuff. I love you Daddy and Aunty Marie-Rose.

My mothers-in-law for the laughter, enthusiasm and fierce love, who raise their grandchildren like lionesses do cubs: Christah Kalulu and Paxina Kalulu. Mummy Musata Kaunda-Banda, thank you for being a bright light and a pillar for all to lean on. My friend and sister Laurane Soko for giving me strength even when I could not see the light. This project started in her home in Paris amongst the love of her beautiful children who asked me numerous questions about our Zambian-ness. Muonga Kaunda for decades of friendship and sisterhood.

My grandparents Simon and Salome Kapwepwe, Elisha and Lillette Omokhodion whom I wish were here. Thank you for leaving us some of you through the books you read, the stories you shared and the legacies you left—inheritance comes in many ways. To my in-law grandparents the Kalulus, the Bandas and the Kaundas, all the freedom fighters and unsung heroes in Zambia, thank you for leading the struggle for Independence. We are forever indebted to you for your sacrifice. We hope to make you proud.

My siblings Natalie, Chimuka, Mwansa, and all our children combined. My cousins, nieces and nephews – because of them, we are who we are – a tribe. I love you all dearly. My brothers and sister-in-law Poze, Muthinke and Buchi Banda, Courtney Rusike, thank you for always being supportive.

My Lagos informants – Deji Adeniji of Soundcity Media – for translating English to Pidgin anytime I asked, and for inadvertently naming the book. Adetunji Omotola for helping me with Pidgin translations as well. Dr. Akanimo Odon, Dr. Akintayo Adisa thanks for letting me ramble on and on.

Super star editors – Anna Jean Hughes, Dionne McCulloch, Jessie Campbell and Rita Ray. Thank you for hearing my voice and making sure to keep it through those countless drafts. Asya Blue for an amazing cover, Matthew Prodger for all the work on the book website, Heather Wallace for the digital marketing insights.

My beta and sensitivity readers – Nachanza Malambo, Denise Clarke, Donna Forte Regis-Muleba, Fadillah KankasaMulenga. Thank you, your feedback was invaluable.

Zukiswa Wanner and her partner James Murua for giving their time, friendship and encouragement so generously. Niq Mhlongo for being a mentor. Short Story Day Africa thank you for the introduction and for empowering us with the skills to tell our stories.

Mwiche Chikungu of National Arts Council of Zambia, Jennipher Zulu of Southern Writer's Bureau, Agness Nyendwa of Zambia Women Writers Association. Keep championing the arts in Zambia. Your selfless work is appreciated. Victoria Chitungu of Ndola Museum your knowledge of Zambian history is endless. Thank you for answering my questions in such detail. Reverend Sydney Kabele of Lubwa Mission – thank you for the tours and the history you shared.

The following institutions: Zambia National Archives, Zambia National Museum, Ndola Museum, FENZA Archives and Library, Lubwa Mission Chinsali. Thank you for having me all these months, for not kicking me out whenever it began to get dark. I will be back soon.

To Graywolf Press Africa Prize for considering my work, and encouraging Africans to write, thank you. To the editorial publishers who almost were – your feedback was fuel, thank you. Christah Dee and Luella Dee – for making me do it. Samba Yonga Women's History Museum Zambia – you continue to inspire.

Pastor Kegan, Pastor Nicholas, Chaplain Kapaya, Papa Pierre Banza – thank you for your spiritual guidance. We are nothing without Him.

Andrew Brand and the 99 Cents family – what would I do without you? Thank you.

Anyone I have not mentioned here, please forgive me, but I will still say thank you.

CREDIT IS GIVEN TO THE FOLLOWING SOURCES

1. G. Mwangilwa, 1982, *Harry Mwaanga Nkumbula: A Biography of the Old Lion of Zambia*, Lusaka, Multimedia Publications, 1982
2. G.B. Mwangwila, 1986, *The Kapwepwe Diaries,* Lusaka, Multimedia Publications Zambia
3. V. Musakanya, 2010, *The Musakanya Papers: The Autobiographical Writings of Valentine Musakanya,* Lusaka, Lembani Trust
4. K.D Kaunda, 1962, *Zambia Shall Be Free,* London, African Writers Series
5. K. Makasa, 1981, *March to Political Freedom,* Nairobi, Heinemann Educational Book
6. P. Sherlock & H. Bennett, *A Story of the Jamaican People*, Ian Randle Publishers (Una Marson extract)
7. W.Sikalumbi, 1977, *Before UNIP*, University of Virginia
8. *Legend of the Old Woman: Life and Customs of the Ila People,* H.M.Nkumbula, National Archives of Zambia

OTHER
- J. Hatch, 1976, *Kaunda of Zambia*
- Dr. J.Omokhodion, *The Sociology of the Esan People*

- Central African Mail, July-December 1964
- The Northern News and Zambia Times Press Cuttings
- AP Archives
- BBC Documentaries on Windrush
- BBC Africa
- British Pathé documentaries
- Commonwealth Digital Archives
- UNIP 1991 Advertisement – You Tube
- MMD 1991 – You Tube
- The personal collection of African and Jamaican proverbs from Elisha and Lillette.

Follow Legend Press on Twitter
@legend_times_

Follow Legend Press on Instagram
@legend_times